DREAMING OF HARVARD

DREAMING OF HARVARD

A NOVELISTIC TALE

◆◆◆

ERNESTO GONZALES ESCOBEDO

Latino Book Publisher
Mesa, Arizona · 2021

FIRST EDITION

Dreaming of Harvard
A Novelistic Tale

Copyright © 2021 Ernesto Gonzales Escobedo

Published by Latino Book Publisher
PO Box 50553
Mesa, Arizona 85208-0028
480-939-9689 | MultimediaPublishingProject.com

Cover & book interior designed by Yolie Hernandez

Cover artwork by Rick Rodriguez

Paperback ISBN: 978-1-7361856-3-6
eBook ISBN: 978-1-7361856-4-3

Library of Congress Control Number: 2021914711

DEDICATORIA

Con cariño y amor, dedico esta novela a mis padres,
Elena Gonzales Escobedo y Ernesto Sandoval Escobedo.
Que en paz descansen.

TABLE OF CONTENTS

Acknowledgements

I AM BLESSED TO HAVE GOOD FRIENDS who supported my effort in writing a memoir about studying at Harvard. I wish to thank my colegas, Cleopatria Martínez and Manuel de Jesús Hernández-G for their many helpful suggestions that improved the manuscript. I was privileged that Rick Rodriguez, a talented artist, contributed the Aztec motif for the book cover. I am appreciative of *The Arizona Silver Belt* for sending me an obituary of Rogelio Reyes. I am indebted to Miami High School for sending me public documents of his academic achievement. Early versions of the manuscript were printed on copiers at the Metro Center branch of Staples, in Phoenix, by the friendly staff.

Preface

MY MEMOIR IS A MEXICAN-AMERICAN NARRATIVE. Mexican Americans have a long way to go to achieve social equality in American society. The leaking pipeline of educational attainment is a reality that explains their experience in American schools. The majority of college-going Mexican-American students attend community colleges. A handful has obtained a professional degree. Less than one percent of Mexican Americans complete a doctorate.

Dreams give us hope for a better tomorrow. But we must start early in life if we wish to pursue an academic life. Learn from those who have been successful in the academy. Writing well will continue to be the cornerstone of academic life. Being receptive to reading in different academic fields is essential to becoming a scholar. The study of mathematics provides a unique perspective of abstract thought. I hope that my story sparks the imagination of those who are exploring life's infinite opportunities.

This memoir is a personal narrative that almost was not written. There is a finality to our lives and time seems to find a way to slip through our fingers. Writers never have enough time to pen that which matters. This tale should be taken with a grain of salt as it is highly subjective with inherent biases and imperfect memory.

Ernesto Gonzales Escobedo

*"This novella is the voice of my Indian
ancestors calling for my remembrance.*

*And it is also the voice of my Spanish
ancestors calling for my forgiveness.*

*I, and the whole raza, owe these two peoples
our lives because they created us.*

*We must never overlook their faults as we remember
that they have survived within our deepest
memories and our daily expressions of passion."*

— Rosa Martha Villarreal, Doctor Magdalena

Introduction

INTRODUCTION

THIS MEMOIR IS A NOVELISTIC TALE of an unlikely first-generation Mexican American who aspired to attend Harvard College. My story is a case study of educational opportunity. Anthropologists have always studied the lives of native people to understand their cultural norms. Presented in the emic voice, this is the story of an indigenous *mexicano*. Falling into the genre of storytelling, this personal account traces my journey to the front door of Harvard University. I follow in the footsteps of introspective Indian writers. Don C. Talayesva, the author of *Sun Chief: The Autobiography of a Hopi Indian* (1963), was among the first Native Americans to write his biography. He spoke of the cultural shock he experienced interacting with the dominant society. Written within a cultural context, this narrative explores how my life unfolded within the prevailing winds of social policy.

Mexican Americans are the largest cultural group within the United States. There are many self-referential names that we ascribe to ourselves. We call ourselves Latinos, Chicanos, *raza, la chicanada, la plebe*, and *mexicanos*. In Texas we are *Tejanos*, and in New Mexico, we are *manitos* and *hispanos.* In some El Paso, Texas neighborhoods, we are known as Pachucos. During the administration of Richard Nixon, the U.S. government imposed the term Hispanic on us —and Cuban, Puerto Rican, South or Central American— as an umbrella federal identifier. These terms are equivalent depending on whom you talk to. Some Americans of Mexican descent would probably reject Chicano as a self-referential identifier.

The widespread armed conflict of the 1910 Mexican Revolution was a seminal reason why *mexicanos* left the interior of Mexico to migrate north. The outbreak of World War I in 1914 created economic opportunity for the Escobedo family and other *mexicanos*; their sons would fight in World War II. When the Escobedo family established roots in Arizona, their life changed for the better. We had to bend and adjust to life in the dominant American culture. The family was starting from square one with limited resources. My parents gave me every advantage needed to succeed in life. I never understood my uneven educational experiences but made changes that I could control. With fondness, I have special memories of Mexican Canyon and Mackey Camp, during my formative years. The reader should beware that this memoir presents one person's recollections rather than a collective family memory.

I am a simple person. My heart is Mexican; my mind is Chicano; my culture is *Azteca.* My political views were shaped by the Chicano Movement of the 1960s. While I value the aesthetics of art and music, I have always been drawn to the world of ideas. I view life through the lens of Chicano/Mexican culture. I am a *mexicano* who is not ashamed of his heritage. A reflective and interpretive narrative, my life was cast in the intersection of *Azteca* culture, Mexican history, and living in a dominant society. My life revolves around the spirituality of *Aztlán*.

I scrutinize my role in the Chicano Movement, which I maintain continues today. I protested society's indifference when it came to *raza*, and became involved in political action through a student organization. Founded as a social justice organization, *Movimiento Estudiantil Chicano de Aztlán* (MEChA) uses the political process to affect social change. MEChA provides real-world leadership opportunities within an organizational setting, and was active in establishing Chicano and Chicana Studies in colleges across the Southwest. Many Mechistas went on to become college presidents, deans, professors, accountants, doctors, judges, lawyers, teachers, business owners, and elected officials.

Affirmative action continues to be a controversial policy in higher education. I embrace the idea that affirmative action reduces social inequality. It is a governmental policy that mandates equal opportunity within colleges and universities. The government policy of affirmative action was first articulated by President John F. Kennedy in 1961, who issued Executive Order 10925. Platitudes would no longer be sufficient; tangible action was required. President Lyndon B. Johnson signed Executive Order 11246 on September 24, 1965. Its administrative expectations were clear: nondiscrimination and affirmative action. Both public and private colleges and universities must adhere to its requirements, which are delineated in the Executive Order 11246 higher education guidelines. Presidents Kennedy and Johnson used the executive order to ensure that the underclass would have a chance at college.

Social mobility is the staircase that leads to a better life. I viewed education as an investment that would improve my life. Somehow, I had to move beyond the socioeconomic limitations of living in a copper mining town. I traced my journey from one of poverty to one of privilege; my wish was to control my destiny. I aspired to become a Chicano scholar, and I sensed that studying social policy would provide insight into the social and income inequality of *raza*. Once the liberal Eastern establishment opened the door of opportunity for me, I was able to navigate toward a life of meaningful work. My personal experiences produced a unique blueprint for gaining admission to Harvard.

Well-educated people have an obsessive fascination with Harvard. This memoir attempts to answer three questions: Based on my life story, what were the perceived sequences of socioeconomic background, family history, and school experiences that lead me to study at Harvard? What did I learn and experience at Harvard? Upon earning a Harvard degree, what employment opportunities were open to me? Every memoir should, at minimum, address the reliability and validity issues of the narrative. Anthropologists have traditionally used biography to understand the culture and society of indigenous people. Textualizing my life was problematic at many levels as my life encompasses a multiplicity of personas. Evoking Jacque Derrida's philosophy, I believe that life accounts have a phenomenological hue; my life story has a distinct hermeneutical quality. This memoir defies the generalizability of *raza* who have earned a doctorate at Harvard in alignment with Jean-Paul Sartre's philosophical notion of a universal singular.

The power elite establishes the social order of the nation and exercises control of economic, governmental, and military sectors. Its members attend private schools then study at Harvard, Princeton, Yale, Stanford, MIT, and military academies. Both the *Washington Post* and the *New York Times* chronicle the nation's heartbeat. CNN and Fox News battle to sway American voters on national policy issues. K Street lawyers and lobbyists in Washington D.C. represent firms and universities that seek to influence government officials. One can listen to journalist and political commentator Fareed Zakaria interviewing them on CNN's show GPS on weekends. Privileged American families share their fortunes with the destitute; notably, the Annenberg, Bloomberg, Carnegie, Ford, Gates, and Rockefeller foundations have been instrumental in attenuating poverty. Comedians wield an unconventional influence by poking fun at the foibles of national leaders. Harvard University professors have written extensively on social policy that affects us all. *Raza* has been mindful of the centrality of social policy and the high-stakes nature of equal opportunity in American society.

Enrique Hank Lopez's book *The Harvard Mystic* (1979), frames how power and prestige influence institutional life. He observed, "In most instances, 'Harvard power' is an obliquely subtle force that functions at subterranean levels, but on certain occasions it flares to the surface as if to remind everyone of its omnipresence." I was inspired by him to seek admission to Harvard University because of its position in publishing social policy research. His chapter on racial controversy piqued my curiosity. Lopez criticized the *Harvard Educational Review's* role in publishing social and income inequality studies that are based on IQ, a measure used to depict *raza* as afflicted with diminished intellectual capacity.

There is a widespread understanding of human intelligence among psychologists. American psychologist Robert Sternberg described practical intelligence in his 1985 book *Beyond IQ: A Triarchic Theory of Intelligence.* He believed that human intelligence consisted of contextual, experiential, and analytical domains. Sternberg did not believe that IQ tests were able to provide meaningful insight into human intelligence. He felt that human intelligence accounts for a commonsense approach to life's problems and challenges. People use tacit knowledge to navigate the ever-changing social landscape. Elected officials are selected for their commitment to serving their constituents.

The Congressional Hispanic Caucus (CHC) strives to find solutions to the nation's vexing problems. This organization consists of 38 Democratic members of the United States Congress of Hispanic descent. Of the innumerable issues they address, the Hispanic Caucus monitors the educational opportunity of Latino students, which has led to the social mobility of many Latinos. The Hispanic Caucus weighs the legitimacy of social policy research where policy analysts have seized IQ to advance a political agenda. There have always been social scientists who believe that heredity is the determining factor of professional and social position.

The father of eugenics, the 19th century English scientist Sir Francis Galton, asserted that the racial superiority of the white race was due to heredity. He was the first to use the term "eugenics" as the conceptual foundation that promoted the modification of human genes to produce a superior race. Publishing *Hereditary Genius* in 1869, Galton noted that the British upper-class were intellectually blessed and their descendants would also be gifted. I have often wondered what Galton would have said about *raza* intellectuals. Geneticists have not been able to explain the success of Mexican-American elites in academia. Policymakers use research reports to understand the nature of the nation's underclass.

To understand the nature of social and economic inequality, the Civil Rights Law of 1964 mandated a national survey. The National

Center for Educational Statistics commissioned James Coleman, a noted sociologist, to conduct the 1966 study, *Equality of Educational Opportunity*. The researchers tested 570,000 students and examined 4,000 schools; the massive report to the President and Congress consisted of 737 pages. Researchers analyzed educational data on the scholastic achievement of Mexican Americans, Indians, Blacks, Asians, and Puerto Ricans. When not considering socioeconomic background, the study concluded that school funding made little difference in scholastic achievement. "The conclusion can then be drawn that improving the school of a minority pupil will increase his achievement more than will improving the school of a white child increase his... This indicates that it is for the most disadvantaged children that improvements in school quality will make the difference in achievement." From its initial publication, the Coleman report was controversial. Rudolfo F. Ramos, Washington, D.C. Director of the G.I. Forum, was the only Chicano to give input into the research project.

The nation turned to Harvard University to understand the societal impact of the Coleman report. Funded by the Carnegie Corporation, Harvard professors Frederick Mosteller and Daniel P. Moynihan organized a seminar that reviewed the policy effects of the national survey, which was published as *On Equality of Educational Opportunity: Papers Deriving from the Harvard University Faculty Seminar on the Coleman Report* (1972). The authors noted, "Here was a subject of such inherent intellectual and social interest as to challenge the best of minds." Not one Chicano researcher participated in the Harvard seminar. Using analysis of variance statistical methods, the Coleman report researchers tried to gauge the degree to which underserved students were academically disadvantaged. The researchers reported, "But there did not turn out to be differences of such magnitude between the schools of Negroes and whites, within regions." What was clear is that poverty has a profound effect on academic achievement. The Harvard professors had several recommendations. "We recommend increased family-income and employment-training programs, together with plans for the evaluation of their long-run effects on education." The Harvard professors envisioned innovative academies, "We recommend that new kinds of schools be developed and evaluated, and that in existing schools new sorts of educational policies substantially different from those of the past be tried in a research and development manner." Surprisingly, they did not suggest comprehensive tutoring centers that are common in schools today. However, they wondered if raza could succeed in college. While the Coleman report was noteworthy in many respects, inevitably, statistical errors were identified in the analysis. But other academics had an alternate explanation of why millions of *raza* belonged to America's underclass. To what end do social policy analysts weaponize IQ to influence national policy?

Arthur Jensen's article on intelligence *How Much Can We Boost IQ and Scholastic Achievement?* was published in the *Harvard Educational Review* in 1969. Many researchers speculate that this journal title is misleading in its intent. The true purpose, many say, was to explain IQ differences among races. A Berkeley professor, Jensen extended Galton's view by claiming that IQ differences are due to heredity. He declared that compensatory education could not help children reach their proper grade level. Jensen noted, "This simple theme, with only slight embellishments, can be found repeated over and over again in the vast recent literature on the psychology and education of children called culturally disadvantaged." He claimed that schools should also consider the genetic background of students to help low-performing students. Jensen asserted, "The fact that intelligence is correlated with occupational status can hardly be surprising in any society that supports universal public education." Jensen discussed the educational intervention of the Institute of Developmental Studies in New York, which led to small statistically nonsignificant gains in IQ scores. The furor was almost immediate when he downplayed the socioeconomic factors in schooling. What was missing was qualitative data and its interpretation that would give a comprehensive empirical account of the academic achievement of the underclass.

The Bell Curve: Intelligence and Class Structure in American Life, published in 1994, was written by Richard J. Herrnstein, a psychologist by training, and Charles Murray, a political scientist. In my opinion, *The Bell Curve* was written to influence social policy that favored the aristocracy. In the Preface, the authors observe, "This book is about differences in intellectual capacity among people and groups and what those differences mean for America's future." Acknowledging the controversial history of IQ tests, they contend that human intelligence is the key to understanding national social problems. Their research used the National Longitudinal Survey of Youth (NLSY) data set funded by the U.S. Bureau of Labor Statistics. Using IQ as an explanatory variable, these researchers present their self-serving views on differences between the rich and educated, and the poor and non-educated. It is not surprising that social policy analysts consider themselves as the cognitive elite.

Herrnstein and Murray primarily focus attention on affirmative action in higher education. They complain about the number of Blacks and Latinos who are admitted to the nation's leading colleges and universities. They contend, without evidence, that degrees earned by *raza*, and other underrepresented students, do not have the same value as degrees earned by white students. Seemingly, the authors wish to return to a time when underrepresented students were not considered for admissions. One interpretation is that they seem not to consider socioeconomic background, which is an important factor when it comes to college admissions. The authors seem to be against any consideration given to underrepresented groups and recommend, "We urge that affirmative action in the universities be radically modified, returning to the original conception."

In the workplace arena, Herrnstein and Murray appear to complain about the way Congress and the Supreme Court fashioned affirmative action. Employers have stricter guidelines that define how employment candidates are treated. To ensure fairness in the hiring process, the authors again recommend an employment test. They discuss the constraints of the Civil Rights Act of 1964. In the end, the authors appear to suggest that *raza* could not perform adequately in the workplace. After a lifetime of working in different organizational settings, I question the validity of the author's assertions.

American scientist Stephen Jay Gould, who was named Alexander Agassiz Professor of Zoology at Harvard, fired a devastating salvo at *The Bell Curve* when in 1996 he updated his work *The Mismeasure of Man*. This work was published as, "The definitive refutation to the argument of the *Bell Curve*." He thought that it was vital to oppose scientific racism. Gould criticized social policy analysts for the disingenuous way they interpret research data. An evolutionary biologist, it was the mismeasure of human intellect that Gould found reprehensible. Gould observed, "Few tragedies can be more extensive than the stunting of life, few injustices deeper than the denial of an opportunity to strive or even to hope, by a limit imposed from without, but falsely identified as lying within." This has been the fundamental problem that oppressed people face.

A graduate of Harvard College and former teacher in the public schools, Jonathon Kozol wrote *Savage Inequalities: Children in America's Schools* in 1991. He described segregated schools and the effects of extreme poverty. He introduced students to the poetry of Langston Hughes that vividly described their reality in his poem "Harlem, What happens To A Dream Deferred?":

What happened to a dream deferred?

Does it dry up

like a raisin in the sun?

He was terminated for sharing this poem with students. Kozol describes the austere condition of the public schools: buildings in disrepair, a poorly crafted curriculum, no labs for the science classes, and students not engaged in academic subjects. He could have been writing about schooling in the Southwest. Kozol went on to write a dozen books on education.

Willie Velásquez, a Chicano activist, grew up in San Antonio, Texas. Later in life, he worked in the Rio Grande Valley helping the United Farm Workers union. He had the foresight to earn an economics degree from Saint Mary's college. He is remembered for initiating the Southwest Voter Registration Education Project in 1974. He proclaimed the watchword *"Su voto es su voz"* to working-class *raza* to underscore the political potency of the vote. President Bill Clinton awarded the Presidential Medal of Freedom posthumously to Willie Velasquez on September 29, 1995.

I was intrigued by Peter Skerry's book *Mexican Americans: The Ambivalent Minority*, published in 1993. Willie Velásquez, who taught at the Institute of Politics at Kennedy School of Government in 1980, invited Skerry to visit him in San Antonio to learn about Chicano politics. Skerry notes, "As Mexican Americans themselves never tire of pointing out, their Spanish and especially Indian ancestors were present in what is now the American Southwest long before the forebears of most Americans arrived on the North American continent." Skerry provides a critical account of Mexican-American politics and appears not to respect the Mexican Americans who provided him a wealth of insight into Chicano politics. Essentially, his study examines the dismal participation of *raza* in the electoral process. When examining Chicano identity, Skerry notes, "As for many Mexican Americans, they remain undecided even when they are not confused." Somehow, he forgot to highlight the founding of San Antonio and Los Angeles and other established communities in the Southwest long before the arrival of European settlers.

Raza has written perceptive and intimate memoirs on living in society's margins and what it takes to succeed. George Lopez' standup routine centers around what it is like being Chicano in the broader community. I admire him for his resolve to prosper in life. Lopez, with Armen Keteyian, wrote the book *Why You Crying?: My Long, Hard Look at Life, Love, and Laughter* (2004). This is a heartbreaking story of a kid who had a rough childhood. Lopez remembers the grinding poverty of growing up in Mission Hills, California, and its demoralizing effect it had on him and his friends. He remembers, "I became a comedian as a way to cope with this kind of wretched psychological abuse, a life so sad it had to be funny." His grandmother was strict and challenged him to confront life. I could relate to his problematic life. With the premiere of the *George Lopez Show* in 2002 on ABC, he became a mainstream entertainer. In 2015 he starred in *Spare Parts*, a movie about a Carl Hayden High School engineering teacher who taught Chicano students to compete in a robotics contest. *Raza* ended up outperforming teams from Harvard and MIT. I always hoped that I would get the chance to talk to Lopez about social policy. His ascent into the upper-class is grounded in street smarts and hard work.

The text of my memoir transcends several languages and cultures. I came to appreciate the linguistic heritage of my parents and *abuelitos*. References are made to the *Náhuatl* language, the Caló argot, and *Azteca* culture. Since my childhood years, I have appreciated the cultural differences that have shaped my persona. When I attend an *Azteca* event, I depend on my imagination to make a connection with my indigenous roots. While I have little fluency with the *Náhuatl* language, I have explored its impact on my life.

I hope that Harvard *raza* students pursue a concentration in artificial intelligence. Society is continually being transformed by technological change. The Defense Advanced Research Projects Agency (DARPA) will find ways to utilize artificial intelligence to protect the nation and serve the public interest. Stanford, MIT, and Harvard will forge ahead in artificial intelligence research that will benefit society. I hope that *raza* continues to embrace STEM fields as one possible response to artificial intelligence ascendancy. Algorithmic driven, artificial intelligence depends on artificial neural networks for machine learning, an evolutionary step up from computer programming. Andrew Ng, an artificial intelligence scientist, considers the utilization of artificial intelligence analogous to the introduction of electricity in 1881. Still in its infancy, artificial intelligence will automate processes in major sectors of manufacturing, art, law, medicine, national defense, law enforcement, business, and education. In time, many people who perform manual labor will lose their jobs due to automation. The information age is firmly set at center stage, but will people be able to adapt to this new reality?

A quarter of a century has passed since I graduated from Harvard with a doctorate. My dream was to work in an academic setting. I decided on an academic career and discovered that there are no shortcuts in preparing for a scholarly career. Essentially, I ignored the cynicism of social policy analysts who believe *raza* did not merit admittance into college. I embraced a liberal arts education that prepared me for graduate school. I was fortunate to have studied the mathematics needed to understand the story embedded in a data set. Growing up in Mexican Canyon certainly influenced my educational trajectory, but I never envisioned that I was destined to study at a world-class university.

"To make a great dream come true, the first requirement is a great capacity to dream; the second is persistence."

— César Chávez, National Chicano Leader

1.

FAMILY HISTORY

MY REFLECTIONS ON GROWING UP IN MEXICAN CANYON give context to my tenuous life journey. They examine the asymmetrical educational experience that eventually led me to become a college teacher. This *cuento* is an account of realizing a personal dream to participate in American life. But it also examines the social and economic inequality that constrains *mexicanos* in the United States. I have an innate understanding of a purposeful life that led me to advocate for social justice. There must have been something in my formative years that led me to take both personal and financial risks to seek admission to Harvard University.

I was born in *Aztlán* —the land of my forefathers, the *Azteca* tribe— geographically located in the Southwest. For thousands of years, indigenous people have lived in this area. While I concede that *Aztlán* does not exist as a legally defined geographic area, it exists as a spiritual construct. The Manifest Destiny doctrine incited the invasion of Mexico, which sought to extend slavery to the West. If it were not for the Mexican-American War (1846-1848), Arizona and the other states in the Southwest would still be part of Mexico. The United States declared sovereignty of the Mexican cities of San Diego, Los Angeles, San Francisco, Phoenix, Tucson, Santa Fe, El Paso, and San Antonio, which flourished long before the American settlers claimed the Southwest. An elder *mexicano* once observed, "Americans never remember, Mexicans never forget." The shift in power from Mexican to Anglo control created a new ruling class in the Southwest.

My life was socially constructed. Like our *vecinos* (neighbors), we lived on the edge of poverty. My parents and grandparents were a strong influence on my life. I was not aware of the assimilative and accommodative forces that shaped my life. I am not an immigrant. Rather, I consciously embraced the obvious fact that I am a *mexicano* and a U.S. citizen. Being bicultural, bilingual, and aware of my social class status, I fully embraced *Azteca* culture that defines my identity and cultural lineage.

In the shadow of the headframe of the number 2 mine shaft, I grew up in Mexican Canyon, a small *barrio* not far from downtown Miami, Arizona. The town is a small copper mining community located in rural Arizona. Originally, we lived at 22 Davis Canyon, but I remember the night we moved to our home at 135 Miami Avenue. As a small child, I walked up the rocky steep hill at night. It was raining lightly, and I was relieved when we reached the small, gray frame house. Dad flicked on the light in the living room, and we settled into our home. This was a time when locking the front door to your home was not customary. The rooms were rather small, and I slept under a rack of clothes. At night I could select my clothes for the next day.

Many years have passed since my childhood. When I have some quiet time, I gaze at an old black and white childhood photograph of my Dad and his brother sitting on a horse at the entrance of Mexican Canyon.

Founded around the turn of the 20ᵗʰ century, Miami was originally a mining camp. During the 1930s, birthright American citizens of Mexican descent were deported to Mexico during the Mexican Repatriation removal process (1929–1936). Families who had lived a lifetime in Miami —and more cities in Arizona and other states— were involuntarily separated by the U.S. government. Many years after this time, I remember Mom and Dad discussing cases of *vecinos* who were forced to move to Mexico. An Orwellian truism, I realized that some people are more equal than other people. Mass deportation of about one million citizens was carried out with the consent of the courts. Estimates of how many U.S. citizens were repatriated range from less than half a million to two million, depending on the source. With a focus on profit, the copper mining industry had a strong influence in shaping social policy, which dictated when mexicanos could reside in an occupied Southwest. I cannot even begin to understand how their constitutional rights could have been discarded. The elected senators and congressmen should have opposed the inhumanity that repatriation had on the lives of U.S. citizens.

Miami is a textbook example of social stratification. Early in life, I became aware of the economic and social inequality that was just below the surface of our day-to-day lives. There were the rich, the middle class, and then us. During the 1950s, as I was growing up, Miami expanded into a bustling community with small-town charm. With its schools, stores, restaurants, movie theaters, drugstores, bars, and churches, the town was representative of American life. Historically, the town was the product of the Old West. Native Americans were the first settlers of this arid region, and indigenous *mexicanos* have always lived in the area. Others came from the East to find their fortunes, and a distinct professional class emerged with very few Chicanos as part of this social strata.

Miami was a boomtown. The streets were congested with cars, and there were parking meters to collect revenue for the town. The Miami Copper Company was located a block from the business district. Residents could see men operating heavy equipment to move copper ore. The company was located on the northeast side of the YMCA building. Next to the YMCA, the Miami Commercial store sold food and miscellaneous hardware. My Mom and Dad only needed to sign for the store goods they purchased. It seemed only logical that I should be able to buy anything I wanted by providing the requisite account number. I was surprised when the store clerk did not let me charge candy and toys.

There was also a busy Mobil gas station on Miami Avenue on the north side of the Miami Commercial store. The gas station displayed a sign of Pegasus, the winged horse. A *mexicano* ran this gas station. He would check the engine oil, tire air pressure, and clean the windshield. As a kid, I was fascinated with the revolving ball in the pump window. Gasoline was sold for 17 cents a gallon in the mid-1950s. Now only weeds grow on that empty lot.

In 1958, Miami Copper Company laid off eight hundred workers. I was a young bystander who experienced the collapse of a copper-based economy. This happened in the context of the Recession of 1958, an economic downturn that spread beyond the United States. Dad was out of work and went hunting to feed the family. We learned to appreciate government milk and cheese. All the families in town had to scramble to make ends meet. When the price of copper went up in the 1960s, Miami Copper Company was reopened.

The copper mines hired mining engineers and accountants to direct mining operations. Many of the elite lived in Country Club Manor, an upper-class community. However, their children attended public schools, where the teachers were deferential toward them. Many of them graduated at the top of their class, validating their social class status. They seemed to have a purposeful direction in their lives. For the most part, their social life revolved around the country club, far from the families who lived in the canyons.

Employment discrimination in the copper mines was a source of inequality that angered many Mexican-American workers. They would strategize in the union halls how to right a wrong. In the meanwhile, they had to abide by a dual pay system and job classification—one for Anglos and one for *raza*. Later, the Civil Rights Act of 1964 eliminated discriminatory employment practices in the copper mines. Landmark litigation paved the way for employment opportunities that had been denied to *mexicanos*. Chicanos have not reached full economic parity in Miami, and socially not much has changed in this small mining community.

The copper industry imported hundreds of Mexicans to work in Arizona. As a source of cheap labor, Mexicans were hired to do the manual labor work at the local copper mines. Life in Miami revolved around the copper mines, and I always wondered if I would end up working in them. Many *mexicanos* lived on the margins of society. One Chicano artist observed that it was extremely hard living in the shadows of society. Life was challenging for *mexicanos* who settled into the canyons. Most of the houses there were small wood-framed houses. In the homes, there was a vibrancy of children's laughter and mariachi music that reflected Mexican culture.

Despite this challenging socioeconomic context, this small mining community produced accomplished Chicanos. Among them, the late Honorable Esteban Edward Torres, who was born in Miami on January 27, 1930. He shared with me that he was born in the Miami creek. His father, a U.S. citizen, was repatriated to Mexico, who he never saw again. Representative Torres grew up in Los Angeles and served in the Army during the Korean War. In 1953, he used the GI Bill to attend college. He was elected to Congress in 1982, representing Californians of the 34th congressional district. Congressman Torres told me that he would probably have worked in the mines if he had stayed in Miami.

Many families fled Mexico during the 1910 Mexican Revolution (1910-1920). The people of Mexico experienced deadly violence on a day-to-day basis. Political and social unrest was rampant across Mexico, which was plagued with devastating famine and widespread poverty. Childhood mortality was over 50 percent; Mexican institutions were not structured to assist the people with social welfare. There were no democratic institutions, and the rich ruled with an iron hand. At the turn of the 20th century, it was ill-advised to live in the interior of Mexico if you were poor. A reasonable alternative to a life of impoverishment was to travel north and work as a blue-collar worker.

My paternal grandfather Abraham Escobedo was born on March 16, 1888, in Mexico during another time of social, political, and economic uncertainty. He grew up at a time when violence was widespread across the land. In his youth, he fought alongside Emiliano Zapata, a peasant leader turned Mexican general who demanded agrarian rights for destitute farmers. I have a fleeting memory of a photo of my grandfather and Zapata standing together. He came of age living and working in Tayoltita, Durango, a mountainous village.

Abraham Escobedo migrated to the United States in 1918. U.S. Census information indicates that Abraham worked as a contract track laborer for the Southern Pacific Railroad in 1918. He worked in the smelter of a local copper mine, and later at the Ruby mine near Tucson. I never knew my grandfather, who died on August 11, 1949, of pulmonary tuberculosis, about three months before I was born. Almost every day I gaze at a distinguished black and white photographic portrait of my grandfather, wondering how he forged his life in Mexico and the United States.

Elisa Sandoval Escobedo de Montenegro (July 6, 2000) wistfully remembered, "One day, Abraham heard that there was plenty of work in the United States – in Miami, Arizona, in the copper mines. He and Luisa decided that they would send whatever money they could scrimp together to Cleofas, Abraham's brother (who was already in Miami), he could save it for them, and they would start a bicycle shop when they finally arrived.

Abraham and Luisa struggled mightily for a year to save and send money to Cleofas. Then the Revolution started. Soldiers would rape, steal, and kill. Losing their small nest egg was too much to risk, and in the dark of night, the family stealthily began their journey to the United States.

Luisa packed a big basket of food for the trip and took only some blankets and the clothes they wore on their backs. They managed to make it to the train, crowded in with old, sick people, chickens, very poor people with raucous children, noise, clutter, dirt. Luisa was horrified. She didn't sleep for almost the whole journey; she kept her eyes on her boys and their possessions. When exhaustion finally hit, both she and Abraham fell asleep. When they awoke, her basket of food was gone. In this condition, tired, dirty, and hungry, the family arrived in Nogales, Mexico and finally crossed the border into the United States.

The train let them off in the middle of nowhere in the desert, in the dead of night. The only thing Luisa could think to do was make a makeshift bed in the sand. To her horror, the ground was covered with scorpions, they were crawling all over the kids (luckily no one was stung). She kept shaking the sheets – nothing would get rid of the ugly, poisonous little *demonios*. Utterly exhausted and in despair, Luisa began to cry and pray. Abraham held the children out of harm's way as best he could.

At dawn, God sent the answer to Luisa's prayers in the form of a track foreman driving along in his track cart. He stopped and took in the situation; although he spoke no Spanish, he could see the dire need of the little family, alone in the desert. Bless his soul, he got back on his cart and left, only to come back with food and more blankets. He also waited with them for the next train, spoke to the conductor for them and arranged for them to go to the end of the line – Globe, a small town about seven miles from Miami.

In Globe, Abraham was able to get them a ride to Miami, and they arrived there exhausted, drained, and unsure. They found more bad news awaiting them – Cleofas had moved, leaving no forwarding address, and they had no place to stay, much less any clue as to how to find him."

Aunt Elsie pensively said of her mother, "Luisa Sandoval was born in Tayoltita, Mexico in 1892 to Pedro Sandoval and Jesusita Frias. As a very young lady, Luisa was considered very beautiful. She took after her father in complexion and coloring, very fair with rosy cheeks and black hair. Pedro Sandoval was very fair, with blondish hair and blue eyes, a pure Spaniard. Her two sisters, Rosaura and

Eloisa were darker complexioned, as their mother. Her four brothers were also blond haired and blue-eyed." When Abraham and Luisa decided to marry, "They made an appointment to talk to Pedro (which was a very daring thing to do). At the first sight of Abraham, Pedro had a fit. Who was this lowly *indio* trying to marry his beautiful daughter? He immediately forbade her to see Abraham again. He warned her that if he ever found out they were seeing each other, she would be disinherited and thrown out of the house." After a long life, my paternal grandmother died on June 4, 1981, in San Francisco, California.

My father, Ernest Sandoval Escobedo, was born in Tayoltita, Durango, Mexico on August 29, 1914. Dad was born during a civil war when Pancho Villa and Emiliano Zapata were battling Mexican President Venustiano Carranza for Mexico. At the age of three years old, my father traveled with his parents and siblings to Nogales, Sonora, Mexico. What could a little boy remember of an adventurous train trip? By all accounts, the journey was a dangerous experience.

Abraham and Luisa settled in Turkey Shoot Canyon, in Miami, with their children. They bought a gray-colored house at 3200 Loomis Avenue. The Escobedo family would establish their place in American society and chart their destiny. My mother admired her father-in-law; with animated gestures, Mom would tell me about how my grandfather would brush out his curls before going to town. As a child, Mom and Dad took me to visit Ma Luisa. I still remember the Chinese elm trees and the massive concrete stairway that led up to the front door of her house. An old-time piano was the centerpiece in the living room. I had always wondered how Ma Luisa was able to buy a piano. While she did not play the piano, my cousins would practice their scales and play Chopsticks. My *abuelita* was a matriarch who ran the household; we loved her and had great respect for her capacity to survive with limited resources. The house has long since been torn down and all that remains is an empty lot.

Mom made every effort to stay in touch with her mother and grandmother after moving to Arizona. Once a week, usually on a weekend, Mom would visit her neighbor to make a phone call to Las Cruces, New Mexico. I would ask her to tell my *abuelitas* that I send my love. After a half-hour of renewing a familial connection, Mom looked happy that the *abuelitas* were flourishing at home. Twice a year, via Greyhound bus, we would receive a cardboard box from them containing *tamales, empanadas*, and *bizcochos*.

Dad enjoyed family life. I will always remember the day he bought boxing gloves for me and my brother. In the evenings, we would box. One letter, dated April 21, 1955, had blood on it as the testimony of a boxing match. On October 16, 1956, Dad wrote, "On this day there took place a fight between Ernest and his brother at 8 o'clock. It was a mighty rough 4 rounds for a while. I thought that Ernie was going to whale the daylights out of his brother. But his brother turned around and started to beat the tar out of Jr. From where I sat it looked like a draw to me. We expect to have another match in the near future." As a seven-year-old, I was not a good boxer.

Examining old photos of Dad, he looked just like a *mexicano* Indiana Jones with a brimmed hat and brown leather jacket, copper shirt, and khaki pants. As a young man, Dad worked in the Civilian Conservation Corps where he helped built campgrounds and constructed stone walls. This public works program helped destitute families from 1933 to 1942. Tempered by the Great Depression and experienced as a combat soldier, Dad was smart, all muscle, and not much fazed him. He worked as an underground miner and used dynamite to blast the copper ore free. For a brief time, he worked as a railroad track laborer in Ray, Arizona, about an hour drive south from Miami. Later in life, he operated a loader for the Gila County Highway Department. I marveled at how easy it was for him to move heavy machinery and timber.

I remember the day Dad built a car ramp in Mexican Canyon; he was always building or fixing something. It was a beautiful October afternoon, and I was his helper that day. Using railroad ties and strong lumber, he built a platform where he could work on the family car and truck. We spent a lot of time working on the family car. I helped him change the oil and rotate the tires of the car. He used the wooden structure to change out transmissions. The ramp could even be used as a parking place.

My mother, Elena Gonzales Escobedo, was born on August 4, 1922, in Fresnillo, Zacatecas, Mexico. Located 400 miles northwest of Mexico City, Fresnillo is the center of silver production. She was born after the Revolution, when Álvaro Obregón was the president of Mexico, at a time when political strife enveloped the nation. With a knowing smile, Mom was fond of saying that she was pure Mexican. After Mom was born, Ma Juana saved five 1922 silver dollars over time. Mom grew up in Las Cruces, New Mexico. During World War II, she worked as a clerk typist for the U.S. Army in El Paso, Texas. She excelled at typing supply requisitions needed to support the war effort. After moving to Miami, she worked in a jewelry store on Sullivan Street, and later as a bus driver for the Miami School District. With a watchful eye, she managed all aspects of home life and encouraged us to study hard.

Mom was a nurturing and caring person who was a loving constant in my life. Physically, she was a tall slender woman. She always had long black hair and clear brown eyes. She was an easy-going person and could have been a runway model in her youth. Mom always found a way to prepare delicious meals. She would roll and cook two dozen delicious tortillas in a half hour. Mom cooked pinto beans in a pressure cooker. A typical meal would consist of a tortilla, *calabazitas*, corn, rice, and beans with a small piece of meat. My favorite meal was the enchiladas made from the red chili grown in Mesilla, New Mexico, and her *chiles rellenos* were delectable.

She was a gifted artisan who enjoyed sewing and spent hour upon hour at her craft. With a creative flair, Mom fashioned vibrant quilts. Their symmetric artistry captured a rainbow of colors. All her productions were colorful expressions of art. From time to time, she would ask me about the mathematics of quilt making. I would help her calculate angles for specific geometric figures.

Christmas was a wonderful season and a magical time for children. Decorating the Christmas tree gave us joy and hope for peace on earth. We looked forward to the yearly ritual of making tamales. It was essential to use red chili from New Mexico. It seemed like a rather elaborate process. Using a hand-held mixer, we would start preparing the *masa* —the corn dough— by turning the corn into a cake-like substance. We knew it was ready when the *masa* floated to the top of a water glass. The red chili pods were then placed in the blender to produce a bright red sauce. The meat was cooked until it fell apart. Then it was cut into small cubes. It was my job to wash the corn husks and spread a thin coating of *masa* on the leaves. Steam cooking the tamales in a pressure cooker was the last step. Mom and Dad would negotiate who would get a dozen tamales for Christmas.

Early in life, I became an accomplished dishwasher. Around the age of five, Mom would set a sturdy wood box so that I could reach the sink. I developed an approach to washing dishes that pleased Mom. I remember the yellow plastic rectangular tub that I would load with a few dishes and silverware. I would pour a little Palmolive soap into hot water. Using a cloth dish towel, I would carefully wash the plates in a circular motion. I used a slightly different approach to the silverware. I enjoyed rinsing the soap off the plates and silverware. What a great introduction to the world of work.

Many *mexicanos* in the U.S. military fought in World War II (1939-1945) to stop the attempt of world domination by Germany, Italy, and Japan. Paradoxically, Russia was an ally of the United States. Every Veteran's Day, the Town of Miami celebrates this national holiday with a parade. The Chicano war veterans, proud of their military contribution, would march down Sullivan Street; some of them limped along trying to stay in step. Their children had a sense of obligation to continue the military tradition of service to the country. Many of the Mexican-American veterans belonged to the VFW where they would share war stories. One town resident was destined to become a national war hero.

Manuel Verdugo Mendoza won the Medal of Honor for intense combat action in Italy. He was born in Miami on June 15, 1922, and died December 12, 2001, in Mesa, Arizona. He was attached to Company B, 350th Infantry Regiment, 88th Infantry Division when he fought the Nazis. His Army citation, in part, read: "Staff Sergeant Mendoza, already wounded in the arm and leg, grabbed a Thompson sub-machine gun and ran to the crest of the hill where he saw approximately 200 enemy troops charging up the slopes employing flame-throwers, machine pistols, rifles, and hand grenades. Staff Sergeant Mendoza immediately began to engage the enemy... Staff Sergeant Mendoza's extraordinary heroism and selflessness above and beyond the call of duty are in keeping with the highest traditions of military service and reflect great credit upon himself, his unit and the United States Army." The medal was awarded posthumously to his family in 2014 by President Barack Obama. The town built a monument to honor this national war hero and the local post office was rededicated to him. I knew that someday I would also serve, but my immediate focus would be obtaining gainful employment.

Solidifying my finances was a constant preoccupation. Early in life, I understood that every person must choose a career to earn a living. I knew that I had to find a way to pay my way through life. Initially, I thought that sweeping sidewalks would be a good starting point into the world of work. I worked as a janitor at the local drugstore during my freshman and sophomore years in high school. I aspired to have a good-paying job, and I realized that a profession meant a higher standard of living. The mining engineers and accountants in my town certainly enjoyed economic security. It was not lost on me that a college education was essential to social mobility.

Far from home, Harvard University was established by legislative decree by the Great and General Court of the Massachusetts Bay Colony in 1636. From newsreels, I became aware that President John F. Kennedy attended Harvard University. But attending Harvard was never part of my educational plan. Attending a top-tier university was not a realistic goal. If I could graduate from high school, I would consider it a notable benchmark. My family was far afield from the affluent class who traditionally attend Ivy League schools; we had no idea what the college experience entailed. Like many of my classmates, my Chicano identity would shape how I negotiated educational and employment opportunities.

Mexican Canyon is a humble barrio but culturally rich neighborhood. Typical of Arizona, it is a dry and rocky enclave. Its quietness is only interrupted by the occasional chirping of cardinals, blue jays, and cactus wrens. In the spring hummingbirds flittered from flower to flower. Caliche, a cement-like mineral, formed the canyon walls. Most of its inhabitants came from Mexico to escape a country in social and economic turmoil. Without exception all our *vecinos* worked at the local copper mines. However, one resident, Rogelio Reyes, Ph.D., was an anomaly.

I only learned of his scholarly accomplishments from an Arizona Silver Belt obituary published on May 25, 2011. Truly a gifted scholar, Reyes went on to earn his doctorate at Harvard University and finished his dissertation entitled *Studies in Chicano Spanish* in 1976. A colleague observed that he was, "...a respected and fearless leader whose teachings and community activities [and] organizing went beyond the classroom into the international arena speaking out for the rights of immigrants." I wrote to Miami High School on July 25, 2019, to obtain insight into his high school days.

Reyes was a *vecino* who used his talents to become a high-performing student who graduated at the top of his class. He was among the 89 Miami High School graduates of the class of 1949; he was listed as the first speaker of Thirty-Eighth Commencement Exercises of Miami High School and gave the speech "The Road to Useful Employment." His senior portraiture was included in the *Concentrator*, the school yearbook, and he was listed as president of the National Honor Society. The faculty sponsor was Miss Gloria Howatt, who years later would be my high school Spanish teacher. He also participated in the Pan American Club, a student organization that was comparable to MEChA. Mrs. Dahl was the faculty sponsor; this club helped Sonora flood victims in 1949.

Many *mexicanos* also served in the Korean War (1950-1953). The *Imperial Valley News* provided an account of his wartime service. "Dr. Reyes served in the Air Force from 1949 to 1952, from which he received an honorable discharge. While in the Air Force, he was stationed in Texas for about one year. He went in uniform to a few restaurants throughout the year, but he was always denied entrance because he was not White. This experience, together with his childhood discrimination experience, solidified his commitment to fighting for equality and social justice."

Dr. Reyes served as a professor at San Diego State University. The Imperial Valley News provided a detailed account of his academic accomplishments. "Dr. Reyes showed tremendous talent for languages and as an adult he gravitated to the study of languages and linguistics. He went on to receive his B.A. in anthropology from *Universidad de las Américas*, in Cholula, Mexico in 1954, completed graduate work in linguistics at the Università degli Studi, Florence, Italy in 1959, did further graduate work in Slavic languages at the University of Munich from 1959 to 1960, and received his Ph.D. in linguistics from Harvard University in 1976. He also earned a diploma in Slavic languages in 1989 from the University of Zagreb, Yugoslavia (now Croatia). His language competencies were legendary. In addition to Spanish and English, he was fluent in Persian, Portuguese, Italian, German, and French; he was conversant in Serbo-Croatian, Russian, Modern Greek, Hindi, Quechua, and Urdu; he had beginner-level language skills in Cantonese, Japanese, Catalán, and Purépecha; and reading ability in Latin, Classical Greek, and Sanskrit. Just before his death he was learning to speak Yoruba from his close friend and colleague, Dr. Lasisi Ajayi, at San Diego State University-Imperial Valley." Under different circumstances, he could have been the founding member of the Mexican Canyon Harvard Club.

Life in Mexican Canyon was rather uneventful. In the morning you could hear the rumble of loaders moving copper ore at the Miami Copper Company. I wondered what it was like to operate a loader all day long. On many an afternoon, Dad would be outside working on the yard. He would spend countless hours chipping away at the massive canyon wall in the backyard. Occasionally striking a hard rock, a shower of yellow and blue sparks would fall to the ground. From helping Dad with yard work, we learned that you must never give up regardless of how difficult the task might be.

When I was about 12 years old, we went out to Pinto Creek on a hot summer day in search of gold ore. The terrain is fine desert gravel populated by cacti. The day was clear, and we could see forever. Dad placed one stick of dynamite in a hole he dug in the yellowish desert soil. He connected it to a blasting cap and strung mining wire about 40 yards from the dynamite. He used a battery to set off the charge, which propelled rock up into the desert sky. After about four seconds, remnants of rock rained down on us. That was a day to remember.

Panning for gold was one of Dad's pastimes. Mom would kid him that he had gold fever. We would load up the old family truck with water cans, picks and shovels, and food. We traveled 25 miles out to the desert to a mining claim he had staked. We would shovel dirt into a rocker, and we would shake the device in hopes of ferreting out gold ore. Dad was able to recover small gold flakes. We were not successful at panning for gold, but certainly, this was a personally enriching experience.

Our street address was 135 Miami Avenue. Years later, I learned that we actually lived on McKenzie Avenue. Mom explained that no one could find our home. So, she started telling people that we lived on Miami Avenue. Everyone in Miami knew where Miami Avenue was. This seemed to have solved the problem of giving directions to our home.

Our small home, painted in a gray color, was situated next to a canyon wall. It was built from discarded lumber, and the roof was made of corrugated tin. Because the house did not have any insulation, in the summer it was hot, and in the winter it was extremely cold. First, Dad built a bathroom in the mid-1950s, and later built an additional bedroom in the early 1960s. He installed electrical wiring throughout the house; he spent countless hours remodeling each room of the small frame house. We were comfortable and happy in this mining camp residence.

Every summer we waited for the monsoon rains to come, and the days became extremely hot and muggy. The rains would start slowly and then turn into a downpour; the rainwater would cause the hardened caliche to crumble. Eventually, you could hear large rocks tumbling down and rolling next to the house. The plants and shrubs would turn a vivid green. After the storm passed my job was to rake the rocks and dirt so the yard was clean of debris.

Some of the neighbors enjoyed caring for parakeets and canaries. I had always wanted a bird as a pet. On two different occasions, I was able to catch a light-blue parakeet and a bright yellow canary in Mexican Canyon. I was surprised that I was able to walk up to them and snatch them before they flew away. I gave these birds to my grandmothers, who loved pets.

My maternal grandmothers left their home in Mexico City to escape the economic austerity of the Great Depression. Their choice to start a new life influenced our family in many ways. Alejandra Garcia, my great grandmother, lived from January 2, 1882, to July 14, 1977. She was married to Felipe Garcia. Juana Torres Gonzales, my grandmother, lived from December 27, 1897, to June 29, 1993. She was married to Eulogio Gonzales. In 1932 they migrated from Mexico City to El Paso, Texas. Ma Ale left behind sisters and aunts; mom would talk about her cousin Javier and my cousin Juanito. I had always wanted to visit my relatives in Mexico City. Unfortunately, this never came to pass.

My *abuelitas* moved to *Escárate* Ranch in Tortugas, New Mexico where they would work. In 2009 Mom and I went in search of the ranch, but never found it. Seventy years had passed since Mom lived there and now many houses populate the area. In time my *abuelitas* decided to move to Las Cruces.

Mom encouraged her mother to buy a small two-room house, which was located at 515 South Mesquite Street on the fabled *Camino Real.* They bought the home for $200, which is a lot of money when you do not have a dime to your name. Adding a room every ten years, the home eventually evolved into a four-bedroom, two-bath residence. We could not wait to visit our grandmothers during the summer. They had a talent for spoiling their grandchildren.

I considered Las Cruces my second hometown. We called Alejandra Garcia "Ma Ale." In her youth, she was a farmworker. Her *vecinos* greeted her with Doña Alejandra. I remember her as a person with joy in her heart and a twinkle in her eyes. True to her Indian heritage, she wore a plaid red, brown, and yellow apron with her clothes. A human dynamo, she spent a lot of her time cleaning her home and caring for her chickens. I can almost see her sweeping the patio.

Entering my grandmothers' home was always a happy occasion. The hallway had a white dish cabinet decorated with Mexican motifs, a red and white step stool, and flowerpots. The living room had a portrait of *El Cristo Rey* with an old lady praying the rosary with her loyal burro at her side. A varnished telephone table and a black Bell telephone was situated next to a window. For many years Mom's picture and Tío Lalo's Air Force portrait were next to each other on the small table. They were so young. For years their iconic photos were there until one day they disappeared; Mom said she did not know who took them. A focal point of family conversations, we all sat on a flower-print sofa. The floor was covered with a purple flower-print linoleum.

I would spend hours on end, studying the *El Cristo Rey* painting. On some days it looked like a photograph. The painting was rendered in black, grey, and white tones. Ma Ale admonished me that the burro had once been a little boy, but God had turned him into a burro because he did not behave. I could not help but wonder if that would be my fate someday.

Ma Ale enjoyed spending time with her grandchildren participating in games. She would lie on the living room floor and shoot marbles; she was a deadly shot when it came to this game. When she saw her grandchildren climbing trees, she would also join in the fun. On one occasion, Dad had to help her down from a tree.

As a youth, I found the *Caló* a wonderful language. This language is a lyrical form of Spanish, a fun and playful form of expression. Mom had a way of bringing cultural meaning to everyday events. In the everyday way of the Mexico City people, she would say *¿Entiendes Méndez? Si no, te explico Federico,"* meaning, Do you understand? If not, I'll explain it to you. *Órale* is an all-purpose expression in the Southwest, which is equivalent to *Forget about it* in New York City. For the most part, *Órale* signifies agreement.

Summertime was a time to hang out at the drive-in on Lohman and Main Street. In the warm summer evenings, the local bands played Chicano tunes. The teenagers cheered for songs like *Farmer John* by "The Premiers" and *Just Because* by Jimmy Edwards. The girls knew the lyrics by heart and sang along. The guys wore white tee-shirts and khaki pants and stood around looking cool; some of them wore sunglasses. I admired the way a sax player gave a sizzling hot rendition of *Tequila*.

The Fourth of July was a special time to celebrate the nation's birthday. We would save up our pennies and nickels to buy firecrackers. The summer night was lit up with the momentary flash of a bottle rocket. Our grandmother would buy a wide assortment of *cuetes* in Ciudad Juárez. I bought a firecracker with the nomenclature of the atomic bomb. Its detonation was spectacular, reminiscent of the historic event at Trinity Site in New Mexico on July 16, 1945.

Every afternoon we would walk to downtown Las Cruces in search of food for Ma Ale's chickens. Walking along the train rails, we sometimes would find mounds of chicken feed. When I went dumpster diving for food, I was unwittingly labeled as a down and out kid. Usually, we would find boxes of unsold lettuce that had been discarded.

Ma Ale provided me with her version on how to become a successful worker; she was a wonderful teacher. She demonstrated the positive attitude and can-do confidence of the Mexican worker. With enthusiasm, she raised her hand to signal a would-be employer that she was ready to work and was serious about doing a good job. I remember the farm workers in her *barrio* encouraging her to join them to work in the agricultural fields.

My *abuelitas* walked everywhere. I walked with them to the Mexican *películas*, movies. On the way to the State Theater, we walked by the *casita de chocolate* that was painted in a rich, dark brown color. We laughed at the comedic performances of Mario

Moreno, *Cantinflas*, who spoke the street language of Mexico City. Jorge Negrete and Pedro Infante were the heroes with stellar voices; they would sing their *rancheras*. And at the end of the movie, they would save the day. The theater had a $200 lottery for the audience, but I do not remember anyone ever winning.

The kitchen was a place where Ma Ale would prepare a wide assortment of Mexican dishes. True to her indigenous heritage, she would start by grinding the corn kernels on her stone *metate*. She would shower the kernels with water to soften the corn. Once she had formed a ball of corn dough, she would roll out the *masa*. Then she would cook the corn tortillas on a gas stove. She would then prepare the red chili by browning it using flour. Ma Ale would add white Mexican cheese, minced garlic, cilantro, diced onion and tomatoes, and shredded lettuce. For me, this was the essence of Mexican culture.

But on one occasion, Ma Ale remembered the dreadful day-to-day experience of life during the Mexican Revolution. She was a young woman in her mid-20s when different military factions were fighting each other for control of the country. While walking down a street, she saw what she thought was red chile. She exclaimed, *¡Qué bonito chile colorado!* When she looked more carefully at the bright red liquid on the street, she realized it was blood from some unfortunate soul who was shot during an urban firefight between *zapatistas* and *federales*.

We were all touched by Ma Ale's spiritual aura. During the day, she would stop and pray for divine intervention from San Antonio, who was the patron saint of the poor and sick. She affectionately called him *Tonchi*. She would light a votive candle for him and place a glass of water for *las ánimas benditas* on a makeshift altar. After a day of caring for her chickens, at night she would sit in her rocking chair and read her prayer books.

On one of the trips to visit my grandmothers, Ma Ale, who was in her late 80s, asked me to help her learn English. I wanted to help her develop some fluency in English. So, we started with a baseline vocabulary. The first and last lesson lasted about half-hour, which I felt went well. Ma Ale was frustrated with the experience; she explained that learning English was beyond her abilities, and that at her age her world did not require mastery of the English language. Then I realized that I had made the process too arduous for her. I should have worked to make the learning experience fun. My other *abuelita* had an easier time with English.

We called Juana Gonzales, my grandmother, Ma Juana. My *abuelita* said that a man should have the Mexican qualities of *feo, fuerte, y formal.* A religious person, on one occasion she blessed me with a prayer in the *Náhuatl* language. Most of her life she worked as a housekeeper for the wealthy families of Las Cruces; her work would take her to Connecticut and Nantucket, an island off Massachusetts. She also served as a nanny in England and traveled to Italy and France. An accomplished cook, she was the personal chef of the governor of New Mexico.

Ma Juana was a masterful storyteller. Her version of *La llorona* was very telling. One summer, in a matter-of-fact voice, she told us the sad legend of *La llorona*, the weeping mother. According to this legend, she was the mother of wayward children who did not mind her. While she did her best for her children, they were very disobedient. The mother warned them not to stay out late because children were disappearing. When her children did not come home, she went looking for them. She would wail with sadness and call out to them to come home. Children are cautioned that *la llorona* might take them if they are out late at night. We were encouraged to behave, lest *la llorona* came searching for us.

After Ma Ale passed away, I always made time to visit Ma Juana during my vacations. On one visit she wanted me to take her to Mexico City. She said that she would be happy to stay at the airport. This city has a reputation of being overwhelming. And I really wanted to take her. While I told her that I would consider her wish to travel to D.F., *Distrito Federal*, I was not sure; I felt that it was a big responsibility to care for an elderly person who could become ill on a long journey. Then what would I do? I knew that Mom would not be in favor of the trip.

Much of my informal education came from my maternal grandmothers. They shared many of the Mexican *dichos*, sayings to make an important cultural point. One day I announced that I wanted to buy an El Camino truck. Ma Ale responded with *Con dinero baila el perro*—anything is possible with money. When a good portion of furniture and keepsakes were ruined by water, Ma Ale philosophically observed that *Más se perdió en el diluvio*, meaning that the property loss was minor compared to what other people have lost. When we had setbacks, we were consoled with *No hay mal que por bien no venga*, meaning that bad times never last. When occasional disagreements occurred, *Hablando se entiende la gente* was germane, that is, communication is key to resolving conflict.

Ma Juana was extremely fortunate that the Evans family from Las Cruces paid the employer's portion of Social Security for her to be eligible for retirement benefits. Mrs. Evans would share her *Look* and *Vogue* magazines with us. I read news accounts of President John Kennedy and his wife Jackie and the eloquence of Camelot. I read about Frank Ryan playing quarterback for the Cleveland Browns, and earning a Ph.D. in mathematics. I enjoyed talking to members of the Evans family as they were always gracious. I remember the days when they would bring a big bundle of clothes to be ironed. I was impressed with Ma Juana's talent to iron clothes so that they looked immaculate and crisp.

In 1970, Mom and Dad moved to Mackey Camp, located two miles west of Miami. With the majestic Pinal Mountains as the backyard, the new modular home was located at the top of the hill. Our new address was #2 Mackey Camp. My parents enjoyed retirement far from Mexican Canyon. Dad would invite me to walk up toward the Pinal Mountains in the evenings; our goal was to hike up to the gate about 200 feet from the house. We enjoyed the warm afternoons and seeing the quail run across the dirt road and the occasional roadrunner. The backdoor opened to a vantage point to view Highway 60, the Bluebird Mine, and the Pinal Mountains. At night one could see the lights of the town twinkle like diamonds. I could appreciate why Mom and Dad wanted to live there.

During the warm summer nights, we enjoyed viewing a constellation of stars. We patiently waited for a passing satellite. Dad wrote a short poem about this celestial object:

> *High among the stars*
>
> *The Echo satellite blinks*
>
> *Quietly continuing its journey*
>
> *Across the evening sky.*

Dad wrote several stanzas, but I cannot remember them. He enjoyed the splendor of the evening sky.

He was an energetic person with a wide range of interests. He thrived in the outdoors and spent his time hunting, fishing, and prospecting. At a moment's notice, we would pile into the family car and head out to the Salt River. Mom would pack lunch for all of us. The flowing river was mesmerizing; we enjoyed lunch among the cottonwood trees and occasionally we would see an eagle soaring up high.

An advocate of social and economic fairness, he observed that economic inequality was the biggest problem that American society faced. He worried about voter suppression. He cared about civil rights, equal employment opportunities, and educational opportunities. When election season rolled around, he would be visited by politicians seeking his support. One candidate for governor came to ask for his vote. In his way, he was an advocate for social justice. I admired public officials who understood the plight of the underclass.

Our family had great respect for the late Edward "Bunchie" Guerrero, a life-time resident of Globe, Arizona. Remembered for being an exemplary public servant, he had a genuine interest in helping people. He served in the U.S. Navy during the Korean War. The Gila County government honored him by dedicating a building to him. The Arizona Association of Chicanos for Higher Education also paid homage to him at a state conference. Whenever I pass by the county courthouse, I look for the building that bears his name. All the old-timers remember his dedication to his constituency.

I have always had a great admiration for the working class of Miami-Globe. Occasionally, Mr. Elijah York, of the Gila County Highway Department, would run the grading blade up the hill in Mackey Camp to remove the ruts that would form after a hard rain. I can see him now, wearing aviator sunglasses, and his crumpled old work hat, long-sleeved tan work shirt, blue jeans, with an unforgettable smile. He always had something nice to say to the people who lived in Mackey Camp.

Nevertheless, Mexican Canyon was never far from our hearts. From time to time, Dad would return to Mexican Canyon to enjoy its quiet serenity. He would sit on his bench that he constructed from wood. You could tell that he had many memories of living there, but he never shared them with me. In later years he no longer would wield his pick against the massive canyon walls. But family memories would always be there.

The public schools were not far from Mexican Canyon. Mom and Dad always conveyed to me that a good education would lead to a good job. For some of us, schooling was the key to social mobility. It seemed that every household was teeming with school-age children. The Escobedo household was a hub of controlled chaos as we prepared for school. Mom checked to see if we had our books and school supplies. In the morning everyone tried to get into the small single bathroom to shower before leaving for school. Urban legend held that the Miami schools produced more Chicano Ph.D. per capita than any other town in Arizona. However, I did not see myself joining the company of these scholars; I was happy to be an average student.

"If schools are our gardens of the mind what crop do we aim to cultivate? Retention of knowledge, understanding of knowledge, [and] active use of knowledge ... taken together might be "generative knowledge" — knowledge that does not just sit there but functions richly in people's lives to help them understand and deal with the world."

— David Perkins, Ph.D., Harvard Professor

2

School Days

L OOKING BACK AT MY STUDENT DAYS, school was a place where I would study a wide range of subjects. We all had a natural inclination toward learning and followed the teachers' lead. The teachers provided clear instruction on school subjects, focused practice on assigned exercises, and provided us intrinsic motivation. They were probably aware of learning strategies espoused by Jean Piaget, the eminent Swiss psychologist. One-on-one coaching took place when students were participating in performance events. Some teachers engaged in Socratic teaching when discussing Aesop's fables. Other teachers incorporated cooperative learning methods. Using a constructivist approach, some math teachers employed elaborative processing. But the ingrained educational practice of the past is slow to change.

Many of my classes were based on rote memory. In math class, we memorized our times tables; in industrial arts, we spent numerous hours sanding wood; in social studies class, we memorized the states of the Union; in Spanish class, we memorized the verb tenses; in American history class, we memorized dozens of obscure dates. But rote memorization is not learning, and at times I was exhausted by the monotony of the process.

Before I started my schooling in 1955, the United States Supreme Court issued the landmark decision *Brown v. Board of Education*, which ruled it was a violation of the Equal Protection Clause to educate students from different racial backgrounds separately. The Court observed, "separate educational facilities are inherently unequal." Racial segregation in the Miami Public Schools ended in 1954, and I was a beneficiary of this judicial ruling. The *mexicanos* in Miami seldom spoke about attending segregated schools.

I admired my classmates who were cordial, talented, and had insight into solving day-to-day problems. Most of us were not introduced to critical thinking in school. For the most part, we were passive learners rather than active learners. I never heard of critical thinking as a tool to understand the complex world we live in. Later in life, I attended a seminar by Richard Paul, the architect of the Foundation of Critical Thinking, where he showed us how to resolve a wide spectrum of life problems. I sensed that successful people have a critical-thinking skill set that ultimately determines their status in life.

My socioeconomic background foreshadowed that schooling would be an exigent experience for me. Most children adjust to attending school without any issues. Afflicted with dyslexia, I struggled with reading, as the letters on the page jumped around. On the first day of school, most children are out of their comfort zones. I left the elementary school grounds on the first day after being enrolled in kindergarten. That afternoon Mom took me back to school. At such a young age, school was an inhospitable place with many strangers. It was hard adjusting to a new routine and unstated rules.

My initial contact with teachers was full of apprehension. Some of them had a nice way of talking to young students. Others were formal and rather strict. I had not heard of the "Don't Smile Until Christmas" rule of thumb for teachers. I studied them carefully to understand what made them tick. I quickly learned that teachers preferred that you were quiet and stayed in your chair. After class, *la plebe* would talk about who was sent to the principal's office and paddled. Most of us made an effort to cooperate with the teachers. Mom said that if I found myself in trouble at school, I would also be trouble at home.

Mom and Dad made it clear to me that attending school was non-negotiable. They assured me that I would fit in nicely and make new friends. I had to make the best of an untenable situation. My parents had high expectations of me at such a young age. I had no idea how important succeeding in school would be to my future; I was not sure how schooling would benefit me. Without having any understanding of the impact of schooling on social mobility, I diligently worked at learning my ABCs. I struggled with basic concepts and was not sure that school was for me. But what was important to me was that my parents cared.

In the first grade, we were introduced to the Pledge of Allegiance. Using simple language, the teacher explained its importance. Facing the American flag, the teacher had us stand and place our right hand over our heart. She said a few words of the pledge and we followed her lead. We recited the pledge every morning; its words have had an indelible impression on me regarding our role as citizens. Every morning I counted my blessings of living in a wonderful country.

In elementary school, we learned to read within a small group. The teachers used scaffolding to ensure we learned basic reading concepts. We all got a turn reading out loud from *Dick and Jane*, a basal reader. With the help of our teacher, we sounded out the words. Using the look and say method was a practical way to learn. Dick and Jane had adventures at home, which had a lush green lawn, quite different from the desert terrain of Mexican Canyon. The family dog Spot and family cat Puff were also part of the story. At home, discarded Superman and Batman comic books were key to learning how to read.

Mom and Dad were my first teachers. Mom encouraged me to excel in school and to cooperate with the teachers. I dreaded the day I had to bring my report card home as I was afraid to disappoint my parents. When Dad looked at my report card, it was clear that he wanted me to do well in math. I could tell that he was genuinely interested in academic achievement. He would skip over art, music, physical education, and go straight to my math grade. He also stressed that I had to do better in my language class. But he never explained why math was important, only saying that math would determine my economic future. Little did he know how prophetic his words would be.

I was in the second grade in 1957 when the Soviet Union launched the Sputnik 1 satellite. Everyone in town was worried that the Soviet Union surpassed the United States in space technology. This reality prompted President Dwight D. Eisenhower to call for legislation that would make the United States competitive in space technology. Congress enacted the National Defense Education Act (NDEA) in 1958 that funded coursework in mathematics, engineering, and languages. The United States and the Soviet Union were now engaged in a Cold War that depended on leveraging technical expertise.

I remember with fondness the emphasis on encouraging us to succeed in elementary school. At the time I did not understand that *raza* counted as a distinct cultural group. One musical activity involved teaching us the traditional Mexican folk song *Allá En El Rancho Grande*. On the day of the program, parents filed into the school auditorium; nervous anticipation filled the air. We all had cowboy hats and colorful handkerchiefs. We sang our hearts out for our parents and teachers. The parents were proud of their children and were aware of its cultural importance. Later I would enjoy listening to Johnny Hernandez sing *Allá En El Rancho Grande*, Tex-Mex version.

My parents wanted me to be aware of our blessings. Dad grew up during the Depression, an economically challenging time. He attended high school in Miami, but he dropped out in the 11th grade to help the family with financial issues. These were dreadful times for *raza* who lived in Miami. He learned from his father how to work and accepted responsibility at a young age. Like many *mexicanos* in Miami, he embraced the inevitability of entering the workforce at a young age.

Dad never talked about his experiences in school; I was touched that he had an interest in poetry. He wanted us to memorize a poem just like he did in school; we had to recite the first stanza of the poem to his satisfaction. The poem is entitled *The Secret* (Anonymous):

> *We have a secret*
>
> *But just we three*
>
> *The robin and I and*
>
> *The sweet cherry tree*
>
> *The bird told the tree*

And the tree told me

And nobody knows it

But just we three

Mom did not attend public schools. Belonging to the 71st senior class of the Loretto Academy, she and eight other girls graduated in 1940 from this private school. Her mother, not having the funds to pay the tuition, struck a deal with the school officials. Mom paid her tuition by cleaning the classrooms after students left the school. She fondly remembered her classes in algebra, chemistry, English, Spanish, and social studies. With wonderment, I have always enjoyed studying her black and white graduation portrait.

In middle school, I did my best to blend in as an average student and never did anything to stand out. I spent my days daydreaming about flying military jets. I imagined that I was behind the controls of an F-100 swept-wing Super Saber cruising along at 800 mph wearing my Ray-Ban sunglasses. At the time I was not aware that the SR-71 Blackbird was flying at the astonishing speed of 2,000 mph. Often mistaken for a UFO, this ultra-clandestine jet flew over the evening Arizona skies.

The blockbuster movie in 1960 was *The Alamo*, starring John Wayne, who was born Marion Mitchell Morrison in 1907. He was a bigger than life movie star who played football at the University of Southern California. At six-foot-four inches, he was a formidable tackle. When World War II was declared in 1939, he was 32 years old but did not join the military. In the movies he played military heroes, including Colonel Davy Crockett, who courageously fought the Mexican army. Movie fans cheered him on as he killed hundreds of Mexican soldiers. The historical reality was that Davy Crockett was captured and then executed. But American history books rarely provide this factual detail.

I came of age during the 1960s. *Theme from A Summer Place* was playing on the radio. The Chevy Impala was the classic car that many Chicanos wanted to own and drive. Students attended traditional schools that emphasized the three Rs. A cultural shift moved the nation in a new direction. The civil rights movement shook the status quo, and changed how the nation would deal with race and class. The country was divided by the Vietnam War, which shook the center of power. Many Chicanos joined or were drafted to fight this war in Southeast Asia.

Of course, there were the students who made the honor roll. Every quarter, the principal would give them a green and white badge to proclaim their scholastic achievement. They sat center stage during the awards assembly. I was pleased when a Mexican Canyon neighbor made the honor roll. I was never concerned about making the honor roll as I reasoned that it probably was beyond my capacity. But I wanted to develop insight into mathematics.

We were curious about the operational aspects of addition, subtraction, multiplication, and division. We did not worry about the cardinality of numbers, and did our math using pencil and paper calculations. While addition was straight forward, we were taught that you cannot subtract a larger number from a smaller number. I would spend hours trying to make sense of basic division. We tried to understand the operation of dividing a number by zero, dividing zero by a number, and dividing zero by zero. We were not shy about talking to our teachers. Our questions about these slippery math concepts would make our teachers' eyes glaze over; the explanations were at best vague.

The fifth grade was a challenging time for me. One project that captured my imagination involved creating a pie chart, which depicted household expenditures. This was not a project for the whole class, but an individual project that the teacher selected for me. I just did not know how to convert numbers into a meaningful graph. The teacher provided me examples of pie charts, which were useful in everyday life. She gave me a lot of useful hints as I worked on constructing the pie chart. The best aspect of the project was drawing the pie chart in pencil. I calculated percentages of maintaining a household. In hindsight, this teacher made math a meaningful experience.

A language arts teacher engaged us in a thought-provoking conversation about the notion that an inanimate object could have feelings and be the subject of a poem. The teacher asked the class to write a poem about a wastebasket, a receptacle near her desk, which I could not conceive at the time. I never submitted the poem as she never convinced me that it was possible. All these years I wondered about this missed opportunity. My completed assignment could have been the following verse:

The Trashcan

The trashcan sits

Depressed about life

It never speaks

It only thinks

It doesn't wonder

And never dreams

It's just a can

Day in

Day out

It deals with garbage

Marginalized

To exist

in a throwaway society

Sad to be

But a mere

Afterthought

A classmate taught me one of life's most important lessons. Richard was an Anglo classmate who I saw every day during recess. One day he approached me with a smile and offered me a Twinkie. What a nice gesture I thought; no one ever gives you a treat like that. I thanked him and dashed off to the lower yard at school to eat my treat in peace. Yelling that the Twinkie was hers, his sister followed and berated me for eating her delicacy. I felt sorry for my friend because this kind of gesture would be a topic at the dinner table. I never saw Anglos in the same light again.

The sixth grade would be a defining moment in my life. National events would rock our placid school days. President John F. Kennedy made a primetime national address on October 22, 1962, informing that the nation was threatened with thermonuclear nuclear war. Almost every person in town was aware of this existential threat. I could not understand why the Soviet Union had offensive missiles ready to be launched against the United States. There was a sense of pending doom. I will always remember the dreaded days of the Cuban Missile Crisis.

In middle school, we learned about the Thirteen Colonies and the formation of the nation in the crucible of revolutionary times. At center stage were the founding fathers George Washington, John Hancock, Thomas Jefferson, Benjamin Franklin, John Adams, and James Madison. In the *Declaration of Independence,* they included the noble precept, "We hold these truths to be self-evident that all men are created equal." Their bravery standing in opposition to the tyranny of King George III was heroic. But we were never taught that the founding fathers owned slaves and had children with them. We would not have been able to reconcile the divergence between aspirational values and reality.

The classic black and white science fiction movie of 1951, *The Day the Earth Stood Still,* made a lasting impression on me. Landing near the White House, the spacecraft causes national hysteria. Gort, the ominous robot, walks out of the spacecraft to await instructions. I was fascinated with the sleek design of the flying saucer. The extraterrestrial being, Klaatu, visited Professor Jacob Barnhardt, the eminent scientist, to discuss the fate of the world. Because the professor is not in his office, Klaatu introduces himself by correcting the professor's math, which is displayed on a blackboard. Klaatu jots down on a piece of paper the address 1412 Harvard St. N.W. where he is residing. Because Professor Barnhardt is impressed with Klaatu's understanding of celestial mechanics, he meets with him. When Professor Barnhardt questions the corrections, Klaatu explains that his mathematics made interplanetary travel possible. Not understanding any of the mathematical symbols on the blackboard, this was my introduction to differential equations and higher mathematics. Upon being mortally wounded, the extraterrestrial being instructs, "Gort, Klaatu barada nikto", essentially commanding the robot not to destroy the Earth. Having a profound allegorical message, the cinematic theme stayed with me. I knew that mathematics would become important to me.

The seventh grade was a time that I had come to terms with issues of race and class in American society. I felt fortunate that a Mexican-American teacher was teaching social studies. But one day he went on a rant about "wetbacks" coming from Mexico to work in the United States. Surely, he must have known that they were fleeing social conflict and economic hardship to brave a dangerous crossing that a river represents. If the remark had come from an Anglo teacher, what would I have said? I was offended and saddened by his remarks. If anything, he should have commended their courage in the face of adversity; he should have encouraged us to find ways to help them. After class, we did not comment on this polemic censure of Mexicans, who could have been our distant uncles, aunts, and cousins.

I was lucky to take music lessons in middle school. The music teacher was focused on producing an outstanding band; he held band practice forty-five minutes before the first class started. I was happy when Mom and Dad obtained a clarinet for me; I knew that the family sacrificed for us to have a musical education. I had always enjoyed the Big Band sound and hoped to play the music of Benny Goodman and Pete Fountain. Every morning I carried my clarinet to school hoping that I would not mess up during morning practice sessions.

When the weather was pleasant, the school band marched down Sullivan Street. On cue, we would play a resounding rendition of the American march *Our Director*. Our uniforms were a turquoise color shirt and black pants. During the Christmas season, we would play holiday music. The public performances I enjoyed the most were the eighth-grade graduations. I was impressed by the graduates walking to receive their diplomas to the strains of *Pomp and Circumstance*.

At school, we played *A String of Pearls*, a Big Band melody. At home, we listened to the Sonora Santanera —a tropical music orchestra from Mexico—, and mariachi music. We had a vinyl record of Mexican singer Javier Solis singing *Sabor a mí*. Later, Ersi Arvizu, lead singer with El Chicano, would transform *Sabor a mí* into an iconic Mexican standard. Little Joe, king of Tex-Mex music, was popular in Mexican American households. It was perplexing that the music teacher had so little appreciation for Mexican music; it seemed as if we lived in two different worlds.

One day the music teacher wanted me to learn how to play classical music. He gave me sheet music for a *scherzo* to play with a classmate. I played clarinet and she played the flute. We practiced and practiced until the day of our public performance came. I must admit that it was a tad challenging for a 7th grader, but I gained an appreciation for classical music. I wondered if I would get a chance to play Mexican music.

After I learned to play the clarinet, I composed a romantic *bolero*. In time I was able to refine my composition. When I played it for Mom, she gave me a knowing smile and said that my composition was a popular French song, *La Vie en rose*—life in pink. Written in the 1940s by Louis Guglielmi, this memorable song became a timeless love song. I enjoy Celine Dion's amorous interpretation of this ballad; Madonna gives a rather poignant performance. While my career as a composer did not flourish, I came to appreciate that I had a creative gene.

I have always enjoyed the lyrical nature of *La Bamba*, an infectious folk song from Veracruz, Mexico often played during weddings. The Top Notes first sang the lyrics of *Twist and Shout*; later the Isley Brothers modified the music and lyrics. In 1963 the Beatles took the music and recorded an electrifying rendition of *Twist and Shout*. Los Lobos, a renowned Chicano band, made *La Bamba* their signature song. Inevitably, the two songs would be performed together as an homage to its Mexican roots.

The music teacher worked wonders using small group instruction. Most days, students enjoyed the chance to refine their musical performances. But Friday morning, November 22, 1963, was not to be a typical school day. The music teacher was informed at 11:30 a.m. that President John F. Kennedy had been assassinated in Dallas, Texas. We understood the severity of this national tragedy. That day a sad quietness fell over the school.

The Lyndon B. Johnson presidency launched the Great Society programs with the goal to eliminate social and economic inequality. President Johnson served in World War II and had been a public-school teacher before entering government service. His War on Poverty legislation was his response to economic inequality found in towns like Miami. SER (Service, Employment, and Redevelopment) agencies were established to promote job training for people on welfare. I considered enrolling in the Job Corps located on the San Carlos Indian Reservation, which helped teenagers with job training and vocation training.

Our most important extracurricular activity was playing basketball. The competition on the court was intense; teams were formed by grade level. This was serious stuff for us. Occasionally the music teacher would interrupt our game to practice for a pending public performance. After school, we played basketball under the sponsorship of the Y. Yet we were reminded to study hard and stay out of trouble.

I was introduced to writing for a purpose in the seventh grade. We learned the basics of English grammar. The teacher asked me to write an article for the class newspaper. He assigned me the topic of my hometown Miami, Arizona. I sensed that somehow, I should tap my creative talent in this writing assignment. There were so many ways to approach this assignment, but I did not know how to get started, since I did not receive any coaching on writing this newspaper piece. Perhaps if he had used scaffolding to guide me through, the assignment would have been meaningful. I quickly learned about writer's block. Somehow, I muddled through this assignment but never received any feedback.

A major life-changing event occurred when I attended summer school in Las Cruces to take a six-week new math course. This was a shift away from arithmetic that was taught as part of the traditional three Rs. We were introduced into the abstract world of set theory. Taught in a seminar format, students were encouraged to ask conceptual questions. I was curious about the dimensions of a point in space; it was hard to imagine a dimensionless object. We were introduced to set notation, Venn diagrams, Euclidean geometry, and the daunting concept of infinity. At that age, I wondered if two parallel lines could converge at infinity.

Eighth grade was a rather uneventful year for me. I wanted to learn to speak French, but it never dawned on me that I should have a native speaker teaching me the language. Simple French words like *oui* threw me for a loop. Always having an interest in biography, I had hoped to read Jean-Paul Sartre's *Huis-clos et La Nausée.* Now I am learning to speak French viewing the film *Love Me If You Dare* (2003) with English subtitles. Marion Cotillard and Guillaume Canet star in this romantic comedy. This is a compelling love story that defies logic where a red and yellow carousel tin can is a thematic object. Julien and Sophia, two children, invent a game of "dares," which they play out into their old age. Their pranks on each other produce unintended consequences. Listening to spoken French is both captivating and instructive.

La plebe, classmates from Davis Canyon, seemed to be well rounded in many respects. I lived there for a brief period. At school, I witnessed one of them make a full-court basketball shot— no less in the last second of the game. Who is capable of such an impossible feat? Many of them were great musicians; others were talented artists; one was an orator. Some of them served later in the Marines and Army. I always wondered what was in the water that made them exceptional.

I was an introverted student and not one to reveal my emotions lest my classmates think I was soft. I sought to be personable and tried to blend into the background. Michael Beldoch, a clinical psychologist, introduced Emotional Intelligence (EQ) in a 1964 psychology paper. EQ transcended the traditional notion of human intelligence and was founded on the positive qualities of empathy, compassion, and kindness. Grounded people think it is more important to have a high EQ than IQ. Middle school students opted to embrace social skills rather than to brag about how smart they were.

I graduated from the 8th grade on Tuesday, May 26, 1964, at 8:00 p.m. at Vandal Field. We received a solid education and were looking forward to high school. Mom and Dad were pleased about this milestone; now there was an outside chance that I could move forward in life. Moving from a middle school to high school would be a disquieting time. As freshmen, we would have to be self-directing within a time-honored tradition typical of the times.

I was oblivious to the passage of the Civil Rights Law of 1964 when it was enacted. President Johnson signed the Act into law on July 2, 1964. Title IV of the Act prohibited the segregation of students in public education. Most of the civil rights litigation in the Southwest dealt with race and national origin complaints as well as age, gender, disability, and religious complaints. Later, the Education Amendments of 1972 strengthened the protections of covered classes. The new legislation prompted Congress to provide funding to study the depth of economic and social inequality.

The summer before I started high school, the major television stations were covering the Vietnam War. Lieutenant Junior Grade (LTJG) Everett Alvarez, Jr., was the first Navy aviator that was shot down over North Vietnam and taken as a prisoner of war. The reporters never gave a clear and convincing explanation of why the United States was fighting this war; the town's people were divided on this national issue. The evening news provided footage of the bloody carnage that American soldiers endured daily. My prayers were always with the soldiers fighting in the jungles of Vietnam. I wondered if it would be my fate to fight in this war.

Founded on academic tradition, Miami High School was the premier secondary school in the area. Our mascot was the Vandal, and our colors were green and white. With its regal Roman columns, the high school was located on Prospect Avenue on a hill above Miami. We walked to the high school looking forward to socializing with friends. Mixed in with upper-class students, who were rather rambunctious, we strived at fitting in. The beginning of the school day started with a chime from the principal's office, where he would read school announcements. On the first day of classes, the principal demanded that the freshmen get to their classes, or he would send us back to middle school. That threat set the tone for the rest of the school year.

My goal was to study and stay out of trouble. I was still trying to grasp the necessity of obtaining a good education. I mingled with classmates from the canyons who encouraged me with the obvious, *Ponte trucha*, that is, be ready for anything. Students from Roosevelt, Claypool, Wheat Fields, Central Heights, and Midland City were bused to the high school. But I had limited interaction with white classmates and had no idea about their lives. At noon I looked forward to meeting up with friends. We had our sack lunches and never were disappointed with the social dynamics during the lunch hour. The students with money went over to Pauline's café for homemade butter tortillas. Others went to Pauline's to smoke, and almost on cue, two testosterone-charged antagonists would square off and brawl to the cheers of onlookers. I never saw any teachers in the area.

We enjoyed the high energy school assemblies. With students filing into the auditorium, the Supremes' music was playing on the jukebox, singing their hit *Where Did Our Love Go*. I can still hear the mesmerizing clap at the beginning of this hit song with its bumping bass sound. Students would stand for the Pledge of Allegiance and an inspirational prayer. The principal, a polished speaker, would introduce the student body president. Then the student body president introduced the varsity coaches; they talked about the importance of sports and school spirit. The marching band would play a stirring rendition of *On Miami*, the school fight song; the cheerleaders would lead the student body in a spirited cheer.

Every Thanksgiving Day the Miami Vandals would play football against the Globe Tigers. High school alums came from around the nation to view this high-stakes game. The game was scheduled at 2:00 p.m. to take place during the warmest part of a November afternoon. There was a week-long celebration involving school assemblies and a parade related to this athletic event. The students from Miami would mess up the G, and the students from Globe would burn the M. At stake was the Copper Kettle, which would go to the winner of the annual event. For the winners, it was a memorable Thanksgiving, but for the losers, it was the worst day of their lives. After the game students would brawl in the streets to continue the rivalry. This violence eventually led to ending the Thanksgiving football game between the two mining communities.

School bells sounded to indicate the change of classes. Walking to the student lockers, the noise intensity went up at least 100 decibels. Chaos reigned supreme and we loved it. The banged-up student lockers were in a small area with little room to maneuver. This part of the school was in constant bedlam with students shouting and misbehaving. Students trying to get their books were pressed against other students. But we took the circumstances of tight quarters in good spirits.

In my first year in high school, an Anglo student, while doing his schoolwork, started a conversation about dumb Mexicans. Not talking directly to me, he knew I could hear his racial slur. The insult was a slap in the face, and I was primed to fight. Thinking through the personal affront, I knew that fighting was a major school infraction. I knew Mom and Dad did not want to come to school to defend me for fighting in school. I decided to just let it go. I speculated that he would deny uttering the racial slur. Instead, I decided to buckle down and do my best on academics lest I become a low-performing student. For the first time, I had to consider how intelligence is distributed across racial lines. Many of the students from the canyons were street smart and had a lot of common sense. Even if *raza* did not have an innate capacity for abstract thought, we were not deserving of the contempt that we were subjected to. I should have filed a complaint with the school principal. Sadly, I remember him as a classmate who never graduated from high school.

While I do not remember the English, Spanish, and Math classes I was taking, I recall a science project that I selected. It involved electrolysis, the chemical process in copper plating. I drew a diagram of the chemistry involved in this chemical process as part of my narrative. Years later, I was hired at the local copper mine and briefly worked at the Tank House. This was a place that was covered in a fine sulfuric acid powder that would burn holes in your work clothes. I could only imagine what inhaling the acidic powder would do to your lungs.

Mathematics is an opaque symbolic language, which was beyond my comprehension. I was fascinated with the Greek letter sigma used to denote summation in mathematics. The additive inverse was an obscure concept in algebra that highlighted my difficulties with language. I would spend an inordinate amount of time contemplating this elusive math idea not being able to resolve its connotation. It never occurred to ask the math teacher for help. Later when I started teaching math, I would tell students that it just means the opposite, that the additive inverse of *e* is *-e* because when you add them the result is zero. They would point out that *e* was a vowel of the English language. I would smile and add that *e* is a numeral that represents a real number.

My sophomore year was memorable; I enrolled in the core academic classes. When I had free time, I entered the public library to explore a world of ideas. Usually, I was the only person in the library. It became my reading room with all the books crammed into a small space. I could spend hours reading a wide range of topics, which included literature, American and Mexican history, astronomy, political science, philosophy, biology, mathematics, the law as well as Greek and Roman mythology. Mostly I enjoyed reading about the great battles of World War II. Somehow, I must have impressed the librarian. She encouraged me to study at Harvard, which I considered highly unlikely. Maybe this could have been possible at another time or under different circumstances.

President Johnson understood the impact of poverty first-hand on schooling. Congress passed the Elementary and Secondary Education Act (ESEA) of 1965, with a purpose to infuse schools with federal money. Title I of the Act was designated to help low-income families; many families in Miami qualified for this type of assistance. The Higher Education Act (HEA) of 1965 provided college-going students direct financial aid through the PELL Grant.

I had a clearer understanding of the possibility of social mobility when I started my junior year. I never was subjected to racial discrimination as a high school student, but the teachers gave a lot of special attention to the smart students; the rest of us were not invited to write for the school paper or participate in the debate team. Clearly, we were not in the loop as the teachers never considered us for these prestigious positions.

I took English, Spanish, Physics, Geometry, and American History during my Junior year. I became more comfortable with the ideas presented in my classes. I was introduced to Mexican literature, and found *Pensativa* (1945), a novel about the Cristero War, to be insightful into the lives of people fighting for economic and social survival in Mexico. This novel was an exemplar of exceptional writing. I could only hope that I would write this well someday.

The American History teacher covered the Mexican-American War from a mainstream perspective. Every student knew that the United States invaded Mexico. He introduced Manifest Destiny as a logical consequence of American policy. *¡Chale!* Really! We did not buy his hegemonic interpretation. I wondered how this incongruous treatment of history evolved as objective reality. *Occupied America: A History of Chicanos,* the highly acclaimed history book on the Southwest, would provide a different account, but would not be published until 1981. The military historian John S. D. Eisenhower, author of *So Far From God: The U.S. War With Mexico 1846-1848* (1989), noted that the United States conquest of the Southwest "... resembled the Eighteenth-Century partitions of Poland or the consequence of the notorious Munich agreement of 1938." The history teacher did not give a convincing account of the Battle of the Alamo. Folklore renders an account of 187 Texans defending the Alamo. In actuality, according to Texas archives, there were ten *Tejano* defenders.

The teacher did not give any credit to Mexican-American heroes. Juan N. Seguín, born of Spanish nobility and raised in Mexico, was a *Tejano* leader. His allegiance was to the Republic of Texas and fought General Antonio López de Santa Anna and the Mexican army. Seeing southerners streaming into Texas, Seguín complained he felt like "a foreigner in my native land." He was the first mayor of San Antonio who was unceremoniously removed from office by the ruling Anglo class. Mexicans had to leave their homes and abandon their business-es. This would lead to widespread poverty within the *mexicano* social class. While many students admired this history teacher, I felt that he never provided contextual insight into the destruction of Mexican society in the Southwest.

James Coleman, from the University of Chicago, participated in the Harvard conference on the Equality of Educational Opportunity Report on October 2, 1967. He observed that free education and a common curriculum of public schools promoted the concept of equal educational opportunity. I felt fortunate to have the educational opportunities that Dad did not have.

But institutional change was in the air. After a scathing article describing the crumbling infrastructure of Miami High School, published in the *Arizona Republic*, the school board decided to close the mining-town landmark in 1967. The newspaper published a photo of the high school with a horse and carriage that was taken circa 1917. Everyone was against the move to a new high school. Like many of my classmates, I was sad to leave a grand school.

The best school assembly at the new high school building featured the mariachi music of the talented *Changitos Feos* from Tucson. They started their musical performance with the traditional mariachi melody *Son de la negra*. They even played a rousing country-western rendition of the instrumental *Orange Blossom Special* to the amazement of all the students. The *Changitos Feos* went on to become first-rate performers at Disney World.

During my senior year, I earned exceptional grades and felt comfortable in my classes. The class of 1968 would be the first graduating class from the new high school. Constructed on Ragus Road, the new building had all the amenities of a top-tier school. I valued the modern science labs and auto mechanics area. I spent a lot of time reading in the new school library. I was drawn to the Harvard Classics anthology. I was captivated by Volume 12 of Plutarch's Lives; Plutarch was an aristocratic Greek biographer. My English teacher quickly let me know that she did not have any interest in the Greek classics. I had other questions. I probably should not ask about Dostoyevsky's insight into the human condition. I had no context to understand this teacher's indifference.

The Class of 1968 hoped to win the big game between Miami and Globe; we did not want to remember our last year as losing the Copper Kettle. Under the stadium lights of Ragus Field, the Green and White squared off against the Orange and Black. The MHS band played a resounding *On Miami*, while the cheerleaders and Pom-Pom girls hailed the team. I knew that both football teams played their hearts out for their classmates. In the end, the Miami Vandals beat the Globe Tigers 40-6.

Robert Reveles, a native of Miami, came to a school assembly to discuss his congressional candidacy; I think he was related to one of our *vecinos*. He had served as a special assistant to Congressman Morris K. Udall in 1968. This was the first time I observed a Mexican American run for national office, and found it interesting that he used note cards to keep on point. His analysis of substantive issues and a polished speaking style gave him a chance of winning a seat in Congress. Although he did not win the congressional race, he served as a role model to *raza* about holding an elective office.

On a hot sweltering day, I experienced a humiliating experience in my English composition class. The English teacher informed the class that he would review a writing assignment. He advised the class that he would critique a student paper on how *not* to write an essay. I was surprised that he had selected my composition. He transformed my written work into an overhead transparency, then went line by line on what was wrong with my composition. This paper could have been a promising first draft. The teacher never sat down with me to explore ways to improve the paper. This was a sobering life event; I was ready to drop out of school. But Mom and Dad worked hard day in and day out to provide us an education; I would just have to weather this callous treatment.

English composition continued to be a problematic course for me. If I were to graduate, I would need to pass senior English. I could only imagine what it takes to be a gifted writer. I was shocked that I was awarded an F on my term paper, but I finished my English class with a letter grade of D. Without the adeptness to write academic papers, I worried that I would not be successful in college. More embarrassingly, the librarian would ask me about my term paper. After a while, she surmised that I failed to submit a passing paper. But who could have foreseen that I would be placed in Honors English at a university a few months later?

While my classmates were meeting with school counselors about attending college, I spent my time thinking about entering an auto mechanic apprenticeship. I saw this type of schooling related to stable employment and earning an income. Without any explanation, I was informed that I was not selected for the auto mechanic program. I was stunned and should have asked how the decision was made. The selection process of students seemed arbitrary to me. Without a career path, I wondered if I was destined to become a laborer. I had witnessed graduating seniors naturally move on to work in the copper mines.

The country was shaken by the Tet Offensive on January 20, 1968. North Vietnam soldiers and the Viet Cong launched a major military campaign to defeat U.S. troops. American soldiers repealed the assault, but the news media had questions about their resolve to continue the fight. The highly respected journalist Walter Cronkite did not feel the American military could win the war. Many Chicanos would join the military after graduating from high school. I felt that young men should not be dying in a distant land that had little connection to national security. Some of my classmates joined the military to fight in Vietnam while others were drafted.

I found a comfort zone with senior math, which was a blend of algebra, trigonometry, and a taste of calculus. The math teacher had a gift for teaching and inspired us to excel. He gave us a nice introduction to trigonometry. My success in math led me to wonder if I could pursue a STEM career. I was thankful that the teacher cared about students. Interestingly, we were told that the country was converting from the English system of measurement to the metric system in the following year. Well, it never happened, and I am still waiting. The teacher was very encouraging and never talked down to us. I was happy that I would be graduating.

Toward the end of the school year, Martin Luther King, Jr. was assassinated. He died on April 4, 1968; the nation was enveloped in darkness. Robert Kennedy met with black mourners and gave a moving eulogy while a presidential candidate. Standing on a flatbed truck, Kennedy captured the nation's sentiment when he recited Aeschylus' poem, *"And even in our sleep, pain which cannot forget falls drop by drop upon the heart, until in our despair, against our will, comes wisdom through the awful grace of God."* This national tragedy incited more than one hundred riots across the country. It was not lost on *raza* that his dream was also our dream. The nation remembered his *I Have a Dream* speech, which focused on social justice and nonviolence as a means to bring people together. The country lost a civil rights leader who strived to forge a better life for people living on society's margins.

Sadly, Robert F. Kennedy was assassinated on June 6, 1968, during a campaign stop in Los Angeles. He famously said, "There are those that look at things the way they are and ask why? I dream of things that never were and ask why not." I remembered how he embraced César Chávez on the farmworker strike, the poor whites from Appalachia, and the destitute black sharecroppers in the South. He cared for the nation's underclass. I remember how he helped his brother win the presidency and worked for civil rights. I hoped that someday I would meet his brother Ted Kennedy.

At the end of the school year, an awards ceremony is held to recognize scholarship recipients. A National Merit Scholar was given well-deserved recognition. The local copper company awarded several engineering scholarships. VFW had awarded a scholarship for citizenship; Sears awarded a scholarship for leadership. I was awarded an $800 National Defense Act loan, which was essential for me to start undergraduate studies. I was sad that the Chicano students were not competitive in this important rite of passage. If there had been an established tutoring program, perhaps we would have done better. During that awards assembly, my resolve was to earn a college degree.

Graduation at Miami High School was held on Friday, May 31, 1968, at 8:00 p.m. in the school auditorium. I could not fully appreciate that I was graduating, and this milestone was an important first step. The place was packed with happy moms and dads, brothers, and sisters. I looked beyond working as a blue-collar worker and had a sense that opportunity abounded in our country. With this realization I had to move forward in life; I did not want to be left behind. I was ready to pursue higher education but had no idea if I could be successful in the challenging academic arena of university study.

Attending a university meant that I would have to reframe how I approached learning. I wondered how I would internalize important academic concepts. In the meantime, during the summer, I would be washing dishes at the fabulous Copper Hills restaurant.

"¡Sí se puede!"

— César Chávez, National Chicano Leader

3

College Days

THE DAY ARRIVED WHEN I WOULD BE LEAVING MEXICAN CANYON to begin university studies. The air was filled with excitement and anticipation. Certainly, I would miss Mom and Dad and the quietness of Mexican Canyon. My parents were anxious about the formidable academic challenges that laid ahead for me. They showered me with encouragement, but now it was up to me to succeed. We all had heard the sad stories of students flunking out of colleges and universities. As a first-generation *raza* college student, this was my time to move forward in life. For better or worse I would chart my destiny.

I could not return home without a college diploma. The pressure was on. Dad said that this was the time-proven way to escape the pick and shovel work that many *mexicanos* performed in the copper mines. He reassured me by pointing out to me that hard work and persistence always leads to success. Mom inspired me by saying, "Do your best," and "No one can take your education away." I would be attending college at a time when some of my high school classmates were fighting a war in the jungles of Vietnam. I thought it was not fair for college students to receive a deferment solely based on matriculation into a college.

While my parents never went to college, they were immeasurably supportive of me preparing for a professional career. I wish I had a proven way of selecting a college major. With 20/20 hindsight I should have majored in English and sociology with additional coursework in anthropology and Chicano Studies. I never foresaw that someday I would be writing a doctoral dissertation, or I would be teaching graduate-level writing. But I never forgot that Dad wanted me to have a strong foundation in mathematics.

The subject seemed rather abstract, and especially when my math professors were lecturing about n-dimensional spaces. I briefly considered earning an engineering degree. Whatever decision I made, the degree had to lead to a professional position. Business majors seemed boring; I did not want to spend my time designing sales campaigns or working on mortgage paperwork. But after a lifetime of dealing with money issues, I should have given accounting and finance thoughtful consideration. Money is important in life.

I enjoyed reading letters from Mom and Dad about life at Mackey Camp. Then I would turn my attention to pressing homework assignments. After two weeks elapsed, I would get a second letter from them inquiring whether I was learning to write, since they had not received correspondence from me. Of course, I felt like the errant son, and would immediately write a short note asking for forgiveness for my belated response. My narrative would describe my new friends and our hopes for the future.

Harvard College was forever on my mind and wondered if I could have been admitted to such a prestigious academic institution; this was a dream that seemed beyond my reach. All Harvard students enjoyed top-tier instruction by stellar professors. After graduation, they would enjoy carte blanche on the job market. I hoped that someday I could attend a football game between Harvard and Yale; that year the Harvard Crimson reported that Harvard beat Yale 29–29 on November 23, 1968.

A good friend, from a working-class background, voiced his intent to attend Harvard University. Although well-respected, the dorm residents were skeptical of his academic aspirations. He did not say what his concentration would be. What did he know that I did not know? I was certain that I could not make this type of public announcement, and feared that I would be laughed out of the dorm if I did. I dismissed the idea that I could ever study at Harvard and was only concerned with doing well in my classes.

Studying Russian was a disastrous academic experience. I was impressed by the opportunities available to anyone who could speak and write Russian. I felt that this was a chance to explore a foreign culture. My family was skeptical that I could pass such a difficult subject. I immersed myself in the Cyrillic alphabet. I enjoyed sketching out the Russian letters and forming basic words and contemplated the dative and locative tenses. I was pleased to have a B at midterm. To my dismay, I finished the course with an F. I barely missed academic probation by a thousandth of a point. I wished the professor would have encouraged me to drop the class; I received a well-deserved ribbing from my family for signing up for this language class.

For a brief moment in time, I considered taking a genetics class. I asked myself what use would a genetics class be in my future? I would explore how Gregor Mendel, an Austrian monk, discovered the laws of genetics. I wondered if I would have to replicate his classic experiments with peas. Most of the guys in the dorm considered genetics a tough class, which made me reconsider this choice. Little did I know that human intelligence and genetics are interwoven subjects, which would be a future preoccupation of mine.

The dorm had study rooms that were in constant use by the math majors and engineering students. I liked that you could open your math textbook and work on a problem set. When a student got stuck on a math problem, a graduating math major would look at the problem and give you an idea of how to solve it. There were no formal tutoring centers that are now commonplace at universities. Many students left school due to poor grades.

By selecting a minor in Spanish, I thought I could learn about the cultural, historical, political, sociological, and legal legacy of Mexican Americans with the hope that I would understand my identity and destiny. Sadly, the focus was on linguistic content. The university offered countless courses on European languages and culture but did not offer Chicano or Mexican American studies. The university was indifferent to our role in the broader society; appallingly, it is as if we did not count as a cultural group. Was it that the faculty and senior administration were from back East? The *mexicano* community was located a few blocks south of campus, but light-years away in engagement with the university.

I should have found a way to move to Mexico City for four years of study and work. At that time, the city had about nine million inhabitants. I would have learned much more studying at UNAM, the national university in Mexico City. I was interested in the evolution of the Mesoamerican civilization that unfolded in the area. I could have spent my free time learning the *Náhuatl* language and exploring *Azteca* temples. I could have enrolled in a graduate business administration program and worked at the U.S. consulate. Certainly, my written and spoken Spanish would have been much better. And native speakers would not wonder about my pronunciation. But my view of the world was rather narrow, and I missed a golden opportunity.

I looked forward to meeting *raza* on campus. I was delighted to join the Concerned Chicano Students (CCS), which served as a support group for students trying to navigate the higher education maze. Chicano students met on Friday afternoons to discuss the pressing *raza* issues on campus. Laurita, Julieta, and Frank were first among equals, and confronted the university administration on a wide range of issues. They articulated our views to the deans about the inadequacy of our college classes. Collectively we embraced our *mestizaje*. Some of the students were combat vets; others were from middle-class families. We concerned ourselves with educational inequality and the lack of Chicano faculty members teaching undergraduate and graduate students. We were angry and surprised that Chicano Studies did not exist as an academic department. I was sad to see *mexicanos* fail academically due to a lack of counseling services for them. Despite the barriers, a few CCS members went to become legislators, university professors, doctors, nurses, lawyers, librarians, pharmacists, and teachers. Some students did not like the term Chicano and preferred to be called Mexican American. MEChA met off-campus and was concerned with farmworker labor issues.

I practiced my Spanish composition by writing to Ma Ale and Ma Juana. In my letters, I conveyed my hope to visit them soon. I enjoyed telling them about my friends and classes; they were happy with my resolve to obtain a college degree. My *abuelitas* admonished me to study hard and not waste a once-in-a-lifetime opportunity of attending college. I always looked forward to receiving a letter from Ma Juana, who often wrote about the daily events in her *barrio*.

Chicano literature had emerged as a creative genre on campus. Everyone was reading *The Teachings of Don Juan: A Yaqui Way of Knowledge* (1968) by Carlos Castaneda, a graduate anthropology student at UCLA. The book described the metaphysical experiences of another reality. Another book that chronicled life in the *barrio* was *The Revolt of the Cockroach People* (1973). Written by Oscar Zeta Acosta, a radical lawyer, the tome focused on the disenfranchised *raza* and their fight for a rightful place in society. I owned a copy of *Bless Me Ultima* (1972) by Rudolfo Anaya. Perhaps one of the best novels in Chicano literature, its richly descriptive language is captivating. Set in New Mexico, this is a story about Ultima, a healer, and Antonio Márez, a boy. Ultima guides Antonio through life's dilemmas.

I was fortunate that I attended a lecture by Rodolfo F. Acuña, the leading Chicano intellectual of the times. Born in Boyle Heights in Los Angeles, he witnessed the struggle of *mexicanos* who toiled to make ends meet. In his book *Occupied America: A History of Chicanos* (1972), he disclosed that he served 19 months in the U.S. Army. His book became a primer for Chicano Studies programs; later it evolved into a textbook. He observed, "History can either oppress or liberate a people. Generalizations and stereotypes about the Mexican have been circulated in the United States for over 124 years... Incomplete or biased analyses by historians have perpetuated factual errors and created myths. The Anglo-American public has believed and encouraged the historian's and social commentator's portrayal of the Mexican as 'the enemy'. The tragedy is that the myths have degraded the Mexican people — not in the eyes of those who feel superior, but also in their own eyes." His historical research was from an indigenous perspective. During his talk, he shared with us that his accomplishments were due in part to lighter skin color than of his relatives. He talked about the importance of scholarship and encouraged us to learn our history. I admired the dean of Chicano Studies and was ready to transfer to California State University Northridge, where he taught. But there were too many unknown risks involved in such a move. Many years later, the Rodolfo F. Acuña Collection was established to provide researchers insight into his life and academic work.

I was impressed with the university library and discovered that it is a splendid resource. The stacks were beneficial for getting away from college distractions. I needed a quiet place where I could contemplate abstract thoughts. I appreciated the large study area and concentrated my energies on academic tasks. I was envious of the professors who had small but private offices in the library.

The math and science classes have always been challenging for undergraduates. I had a clear and logical plan to succeed in my classes. I made it a point to attend class on time, sit in the front row, take copious notes, and ask for clarification from the professor when I did not understand. My professors appreciated my efforts to learn the content and pass their classes. I availed myself of their office hours. In the late 1960s, there were no STEM support services to help students.

My first English professor spent his time writing poetry. When I mentioned *Paradise Lost*, he just started laughing; I was taken aback by my instructor's arrogance. This classic poem made me appreciate John Milton as a truly gifted writer. Although I was in an Honors English class, I needed a comprehensive explanation of the writing process. I saw writing as an essential academic skill, and regret that I never enrolled in an intermediate English composition course. From a pragmatic point, I should have hired a writing coach, but money was tight.

My goal was to pass my classes and hopefully learning would follow. Learning requires an effort that leads to understanding. While I took detailed notes in class, I never distilled them into meaningful concepts. I never asked myself what the overarching point the professor was trying to make. I never constructed a conceptual map of the subject matter. It was not until I was studying at Harvard that I started recording lectures, which allowed me to internalize important concepts. Over time the cassette tapes deteriorated to a point where they were no longer functional.

During the summer of 1969, I was working in a copper mine. On my day off I joined countless Americans across the nation to watch the lunar landing on July 20th. The world audience was estimated at half a billion people watching TV or listening to the radio. Apollo 11 orbited the moon until it could launch the Eagle lunar craft. Ma Ale, who was born in 1882, confided in me that she did not believe that man had walked on the moon. I could understand her disbelief; she had a nineteenth-century world view. I will never forget the national excitement of astronaut Neil Armstrong walking on the moon. This event inspired me and spurred my interest in science and math. More importantly, I internalized Gene Kranz's, NASA engineer, dictum, "Failure is not an option." This was a time when I was seeing friends dropping out of school; I could only speculate that they did not have the money to pay the tuition.

Returning to college, the anti-war demonstrations were rocking colleges and universities across the nation. The reason for fighting a war in Vietnam centered on the Domino Theory, which postulated that Asian countries would topple like dominoes if Communism was not stopped. If you were a freshman or sophomore student, you were required to enroll in the Reserve Officer Training Corps. The dorm TV lounge was the focal point for watching the daily coverage of the Vietnam War. When the military helicopters landed, the blood-soaked bodies of American servicemembers were unloaded. You could hear a pin drop and sense the silent anger of my classmates. I empathized with the soldiers who came from poor families, while the middle-class families sent their children to college. The combat vets at the university, who had served in Vietnam, only wanted to get on with their lives and avoid heated arguments.

Every night, when I fell asleep, my dreams consisted of fighting in the jungles of Vietnam. I would be walking point and could hear the firefights in the distance and see bright flashes from bombs exploding. Then suddenly, I was being chased by thirty-five North Vietnam regular soldiers up and down steep hills. Bullets were whizzing over my head; I sensed that I was going to die. After I was cornered, I would die in a hail of bullets. What an existential nightmare; I would wake up drenched in sweat. In the morning I would count my blessings and remember my high school classmates who died in Vietnam. Of the 58,220 casualties of the Vietnam War, it is estimated that 5,000 of them were *raza*.

Every male at the university had a college deferment from the military draft. The national debate on the war led to a lottery system that replaced the deferment system. One day after classes the dorm lobby was full of residents talking about their lottery numbers. Some were ecstatic for drawing a high number; others were crying for drawing a low number. They were resigned to getting their draft notice in the mail knowing that in all likelihood they would be going to Vietnam. Because my lottery number was 348, I was relieved that I would not be drafted.

A cultural shift for American society, the Woodstock Festival, was held in New York from August 15 through 17, 1969. With a decidedly sharp edge, it would define a counterculture generation. We were listening to Carlos Santana, Jimi Hendrix, Janis Joplin, Blue Cheer, Iron Butterfly, and Cream. The center of the world was now the Haight-Ashbury district in San Francisco, home of free love and psychedelic experiences. Ubiquitous on college campuses was the classic Chicano rock and roll song *Wooly Bully*, which was written and sung by Domingo Samudio. In my humanities class, we were listening to *Moonlight Sonata, La Boehme, Étude 3 in E major Op. 110 No. 3, Bolero, La Campanella, and Duettino Sull'aria Le nozze di Figaro.*

Arthur Jensen, a UC Berkeley professor, launched the national debate over the distribution of intelligence among racial groups in 1969. The *Harvard Educational Review* published his article *How Much Can We Boost IQ and Educational Achievement?*, which set the stage for experts in social policy and psychology to collect and analyze data on educational achievement. His initial criticism was devastating: "The chief goal of compensatory education—to remedy the educational lag of disadvantaged children and thereby narrow the achievement gap between 'minority' and 'majority' pupils—has been utterly unrealized in any of the large compensatory education programs that have been evaluated so far." He cited the Coleman report, mandated by the Civil Rights Act of 1964, to give validity to his claims. It became an environment versus heredity policy issue.

At the beginning of my sophomore year, I noticed that students had a new attitude about life. We had entered the Age of Aquarius. While working away on math, I would listen to Santana's *Evil Ways* hour upon hour; music which can only be described as magical. The guys in the dorm would argue with me that Santana was not Mexican American. I pointed out that Santana was born in Mexico and lived in San Francisco. Then there was Little Joe, who sang Tex-Mex melodies. His music gave meaning to life on campus. And, of course, many students listened to country-western music. I listened to Doug Sahm who played earthy ballads like *I Can't Go Back Austin* and *Cowboy Peyton Place*. He could pivot on a dime and sing a beautiful rendition of *Ya no llores*, originally performed by *Norteño* Mexican singer Cornelio Reyna and lead vocalist for *Los Relámpagos del Norte*. Doug Sahm died on November 18, 1999, leaving a legacy of great Chicano and Country-Western music.

Math classes were a trial by fire for me and countless other undergraduates. I would continue taking calculus classes with the knowledge that it was the key to understanding the natural world. At the beginning of the semester, the math classes were full. One had to catch the math concepts on the fly. There was not any tutoring center to get help with the homework. At the end of every semester, only four or five students would finish a math class. I regret that I did not master the math classes before moving up the ladder of difficulty.

Today we live in a Golden Age of math instruction where students can get mathematics instruction in different venues. Fortunately, students now have the Khan Academy and other YouTube instruction that help students learn mathematics. Students can watch a ten-minute presentation as many times as necessary until the math concept is internalized. Coursera.org offers online instruction from Ivy League colleges and universities. Almost free higher education is available through Harvard and MIT edX courses. *Harvard Magazine* (June 29, 2021) announced the sale of edX to U2, an educational digital firm, for $800 million. Having gained acceptance, thousands of college students are studying online.

I was looking forward to the start of my junior year. I felt more comfortable in selecting my math classes. I would be studying differential equations. Both Isaac Newton and Gottfried Leibniz, 17th-century mathematicians, advanced the study of differential equations. I was intrigued by the notion that a class of functions could be the solution set for a differential equation. Using pencil and paper, I carefully mapped their graphs. Later I would use Microsoft Excel to solve and construct graphs of these equations. I wondered how Mexican mathematicians approached these equations.

Notable Chicano leaders visited Arizona universities. On October 14, 1970, Rodolfo 'Corky' Gonzales made a major speech at Arizona State University. He was an activist, political organizer, and poet, and believed in Nationalism that empowered *raza*. He advocated for free education from kindergarten through college. He felt that *mexicanos* had a right that Spanish be their first language and English as the second language. He noted that Chicanos who did not stand up for their cultural values were part of the problem. Certainly, I admired his outspoken style.

Distinguished *L.A. Times* journalist Ruben Salazar died August 29, 1970. Caught in the crossfire during the National Chicano Moratorium March against the Vietnam War, he was killed by a tear-gas projectile shot by a Sheriff's deputy. Many *raza* Angelinos asserted that the Los Angeles County Sheriff's Department murdered him. At the young age of 42, he died in the Silver Dollar Bar in East Los Angeles. He was born in Juarez, Mexico, but came of age in El Paso, Texas. Salazar was the first Mexican-American reporter for the *L.A. Times* who once commented, "There's no such thing as a real Mexican-American. The hyphen strips both words of meaning." His life revolved around engaging American society and chronicling Chicano life as it was unfolding in Los Angeles. He reported on the Chicano soldiers fighting in Vietnam. Commenting on societal division, he once wrote, "Why do I always have to apologize to Americans for Mexicans?" His death personally touched me. For a moment in time, I considered changing my major to journalism.

A 1971 article in the *Atlantic Monthly* entitled *I.Q.* by Richard J. Herrnstein caught my attention at the college bookstore. He posed a thoughtful question, "Is IQ a measure of inborn ability, or is it the outcome of experience and learning? Can we tell if there are ethnic or racial differences in intelligence, and if so, whether they depend on nature or nurture?" After providing a chronological view of I.Q., Herrnstein gave homage to Arthur Jensen's study *How Much Can We Boost I.Q. and Scholastic Achievement?* Jensen claimed that heredity accounts for 80 percent of an individual's intelligence. I wondered how IQ and job performance are correlated.

The reason I attended college was to become competitive in the job market, and saw the credential as a means of social mobility. I never considered IQ important in the job market. However, in 1965, Duke Power Company in North Carolina introduced IQ tests to screen its applicants. On March 8, 1971, in the court case *Griggs v. Duke Power Company*, the Supreme Court ruled that this testing was unconstitutional as it had a disparate impact on Black applicants. The Court ruled that testing had to be reasonably related to the assigned work.

On a nationally televised broadcast on August 15, 1971, President Richard Nixon announced that the United States was taken off the gold standard to attenuate inflation and thwart international currency speculation. Also, he inaugurated a temporary price freeze on commodities. He intended to stabilize the dollar and advocated a new international monetary system. I was struggling financially and worried that the dollar would become worthless, then what would I do? The American economy is now operating on fiat, or government-backed, currency.

As an undergraduate, I excelled at university service. In 1972, I was elected to the student senate and served on the student speakers' bureau. This student organization had thousands of dollars to spend on student-sponsored speakers. I was instrumental in bringing Jerome Bruner, the noted Harvard psychologist, to speak at the university. At the time I was reading his book *On Knowing: Knowledge of the Left Hand* (1965), which looked at feelings and intuition. He had an international reputation for his work on cognition. I called him in Britain and agreed to his speaking fee. The business office had to send him a check before he made travel arrangements. He spoke to an auditorium full of students and professors on his view on education. A group of students invited him to the Grand Canyon; I was not able to make the trip to the Grand Canyon, and hoped that his trip to Arizona was memorable.

Professor Angela Davis made the evening news in 1970 when she was charged with kidnapping and murder. Newspapers published sensational accounts of her ties to the Black Panther Party. President Nixon called her a terrorist, and the FBI placed her on the top "Ten Most Wanted Fugitives" list. After her arrest, she said, "I now declare publicly before the court, before the people of this country that I am innocent of all charges which have been leveled against me by the state of California." Her imprisonment did not go unnoticed. A national campaign was launched to secure her freedom. On June 4, 1972, she was found not guilty of the charges made against her.

Despite her controversial reputation, the student speaker's bureau invited her to speak at the university. An avowed Communist, who espoused Marxist views, there was excitement in the air when Dr. Davis arrived on campus. After earning her doctorate at Humboldt University in East Berlin, she accepted an appointment as a philosophy professor at UCLA. As a celebrity, she would be a stellar speaker. She filled the university auditorium and gave an eloquent speech on the liberation of the oppressed. I am not a socialist, Marxist, or communist; however, I believe that our country must help those who live in the margins of society.

After Dr. Davis' speech, the speaker's bureau hosted a dinner to acknowledge her public performance. Sitting next to her I was in awe of this philosopher but was lost for words. How do you hold a conversation with someone who has studied at the Sorbonne? In a respectful and understated manner, she asked me about my undergraduate studies. She seemed impressed when I mentioned I was a math major. She went on to have a fruitful teaching career at the University of California, Santa Cruz.

As an undergraduate student, I had hoped to take classes from Chicano professors. I wrote a letter to the college dean indicating that I would like to meet with him to discuss academic issues that were impacting students. He was a distinguished white-haired professor, who I would get to know quite well. I had always admired him for his capacity to write inspiring essays. He invited me to serve on a student advisory council. I stated that students hoped that the university would diversify its faculty ranks. The dean observed that there were not many Chicanos with a doctorate to teach at the university level.

When one of my *colegas* finished his dissertation, I met with the dean and requested that the dean appoint him to the faculty. A window of opportunity was open for diversifying the university faculty ranks. I wielded a good amount of influence as a student senator, and the dean could not ignore my request. The dean said he would take my request under advisement; the university had been criticized for not hiring Chicano professors. After discussing this potential flash-point with his inner circle, the dean saw the value of hiring a professor from the Mexican-American community. At a follow-up meeting, the dean informed me that my nominee would be teaching at the university.

My senior year was a challenging year for me. I selected The Treaty of Guadalupe Hidalgo as the topic of my senior thesis. I needed to understand the perspective of *mexicanos* on losing a large portion of sovereign Mexican territory to an invading force. In the small town of Guadalupe Hidalgo, outside of Mexico City, the terms to end the Mexican-American War were signed between Mexican officials and Nicholas Trist on February 2, 1848. The war could not have been avoided. It was obvious to me that two nations with vastly different cultures and different languages could not resolve their disagreements without armed conflict. Examining government documents, the treaty was written in English and Spanish. President James K. Polk incited war against Mexico in 1846; Zachary Taylor, an Army general, led the invading American troops. Deliberately, the United States failed to abide by the terms and conditions of the treaty. I never learned why Mexican officials never sued the United States for violating the terms of surrender. My *colegas* were not interested in discussing this depressing episode of Mexican history. My undergraduate research would serve as a basis for the third chapter of my dissertation.

I looked forward to enrolling in a history of mathematics course. I spent hours reading about the initial spadework by Neanderthal man circa 50,000 B.C. to advances on the continuum hypothesis. I was surprised that the author of my textbook was able to pack all the important math milestones into a six-hundred-page book. Try as I might, I was not able to internalize all the major mathematical advances. These days I devote fifteen minutes to reading the history of mathematics textbooks when I remember.

I continued my studies of non-Euclidean geometry and Spanish literature. I had only twenty credits to complete to graduate. It seemed like I had hit a wall; I was tired and was not sure if I would be graduating. As I contemplated dropping out of school, I knew that the alternative was unacceptable to me. At the end of my senior year, I was selected as an outstanding university student and was awarded the Phi Delta Kappa award on May 11, 1973. In one of our final conversations, the dean remarked that I should continue my studies at Harvard.

Conversations with friends would inevitably turn to Harvard and graduation. We were never able to resolve the details of how to gain admission to Harvard and pay the high-priced tuition. I speculated that students from the lower economic strata were not admitted to Ivy League colleges and universities. I had an evolving sense of how the national elite prepared for a profession. It seemed that my desire to study at Harvard was merely a pipe dream.

Mom and Dad were happy that I was graduating from college. Every year Mexican-American parents look forward to college and university commencement ceremonies. A joyful occasion for me and my family, I graduated May 19, 1973, with a bachelor's degree. I was the first in my family to attend college and graduate. Luckily, I was a persistent student and I never lost sight of the importance of moving forward in life. In life it is not enough just to earn college credits;

I wished I had dedicated myself to mastery learning. Moving away from blue-collar jobs was a life transition for me.

After I graduated, I came across a disturbing article, *The High Cost of Thinking the Unthinkable* by Berkeley Rice, published in the December 1973 issue of *Psychology Today* magazine. It was an unapologetic defense of Arthur Jensen, Richard Herrnstein, William Shockley, and Hans Eysenck. Rice chronicled that the national student activist organization Students for a Democratic Society (SDS) labeled Jensen as a racist, and at Harvard people were demanding that Herrnstein be fired. Shockley, the Nobel Laureate in physics, was obsessed with dysgenics; his views were dismissed as racist. But Hans J. Eysenck, a British psychologist, was attacked by students who did not agree with his views on race and genetics. At the end of his article, Rice cautioned, "Whatever the cause of alarm, condemning those who publish unpopular conclusions and subjecting them to personal abuse will hardly settle the issue." His defense of these controversial professors laid in the tenets of academic freedom. In my opinion, he should have also written about the incalculable social harm caused by these professors.

In 1974, the nation was in the throes of the Watergate scandal and President Nixon resigned in August. I was convinced that colleges and universities were not mindful of the academic inequality that *raza* college students encounter. Perhaps this disparity compelled Congress to respond. The Equal Educational Opportunity Act (EEOA) was passed on August 21, 1974, to clarify the intent of the Civil Rights Law of 1964. EEOA mandated that "...denial of equal educational opportunity was prohibited." More specifically, students who did not speak English were to be accommodated.

I looked forward to teaching in public schools. I made a big financial investment in an undergraduate degree, and I had negotiated many bureaucratic hurdles to get a teaching certificate. I taught junior high mathematics for five years in public schools. With fundraising by students, we bought a TRS-80 computer; I taught interested students how to program in BASIC. Because teaching is considered a profession, I thought I would be earning a good salary. I was surprised that teachers are not paid very much. It felt like I was working for minimum wage. With a degree in hand, I was barely surviving financially.

This reality opened my eyes to pursuing a master's degree part-time. I looked forward to attending graduate school as a means of obtaining a better-paying job. I focused on coursework that would make me competitive working at a college or university. I had always wanted to work in the higher education sector; I could visualize helping students select college classes that would prepare them for the future. Perhaps I could become a college teacher. After six-years of part-time study, I finished a master's degree on December 31, 1979. I had moved up one rung on the academic ladder and wondered about enrolling in a doctoral program.

Pursuing the doctorate was more a pipe dream than anything else. Occasionally, I wondered what it would be like to study at Harvard. I had no information about this top-tier school. My graduate work was more administrative-oriented than academic. I had hoped that I could work in an admissions office someday. Because I did not have the money to pay the Harvard tuition, it seemed like a waste of time to apply to an expensive and selective institution. My more immediate concerns centered on making a living.

The 1970s ended on a tentative note for *mexicanos*. The Coors Company launched the Decade of the Hispanic public relations campaign. Set against a black background, a flickering vesper candle, intimated hope for *raza.* I was skeptical about this new beginning for Latino engagement as few Chicanos had achieved economic security. And many of us were wondering whether we would achieve our life goals. Corporate America had made promises in the past and we could only hope for a better tomorrow.

In 1975, I went on an excursion to *Ciudad Chihuahua,* a city in the northwestern Mexican state of Chihuahua. I wanted to experience firsthand the rich culture and history of the region. My imagination took me to the time when Pancho Villa battled the *federales.* I imagined that I was a soldier fighting for the campesino underclass. I met many memorable people who were generous and welcoming. I considered continuing my journey to Parral, where Pancho Villa had lived and died. His given name was José Doroteo Arango Arámbula, who ascended to a legendary status of bandit and revolutionist. On my return to the United States, I showed my birth certificate to a customs agent. But the border customs agent refused to allow me to enter the United States. Even after I protested, the agent remained inflexible. It was snowing lightly; I stood there not knowing what to do. After a few hours, the border customs agent changed his mind and let me continue my journey home.

In 1975, the federal government changed the classification of Mexican Americans to Hispanic. The Hispanicization of Mexican Americans was problematic at many levels. My *vecinos* in Mexican Canyon would have thought I was being pretentious and aloof if I ever said I was Hispanic. Mechistas to this day decry this ambivalent term. The Census Bureau was pressured to update its categories that were criticized as being racists. This new category was conceived by the Ad Hoc Committee on Racial and Ethnic Definitions. A federal employee explained to a *Washington Post* reporter, "I was called a 'wetback,' a 'Mexkin' and a 'dirty Mexkin'..." She was tired of the word 'Mexican' which was used as a racial slur; she felt that the Mexican descriptor had been weaponized to demean people. I knew the feeling and understood her point of view. We all had been subjected to contemptuous treatment, but I never would have imagined that the government would categorize me as Hispanic. But in my heart, I will always be *raza*.

After having time to reflect on my undergraduate years, it is a false economy to rush completing math courses. It is essential to have a solid foundation in freshman classes. My goal was to complete as many classes as quickly as possible for the math degree. Although I earned an A in calculus, I had a fragile understanding of the subject. I did not engage in generative performances that Harvard Professor David Perkins says leads to students extrapolating "beyond what they know." He proposes that learners build mental models of subjects they study within the parameters of breadth, coherence, generativity, and accessibility. It would be helpful to have had this insight as a structured way of learning.

I had resolved to serve in the military. I had to do my part given the sacrifices that Dad and my *tíos* made during World War II. During the 1980s the Soviet and U.S. tensions were at their peak. Movies like *Fail Safe* (1964) depicted since the early sixties the consequences of nuclear war between the two nations. This military scenario was not premised on the implausible reasons for fighting a war in Southeast Asia. But time was running out for me; I had to enlist before my 34th birthday due to an Army age restriction. With war looming on the horizon, now was the time to serve as a soldier.

"You know, there's a saying among us veterans, 'For those who have fought for it, life has a special flavor the protected will never know.'"

— MSG Roy Benavidez, 82nd Airborne Ranger,
Medal of Honor Recipient

4

MILITARY SERVICE

SERVING IN THE MILITARY WAS A DISTINCT PRIVILEGE for me. Mexican Americans have always stepped forward to serve their country as *soldados*, and I was not going to miss out on this obligation. On January 20, 1982, I entered service as a Private First Class. My enlistment document noted, "As a new member of the Volunteer Army, you have demonstrated keen foresight by accepting the Army's challenge." I looked forward to serving in the combat arms as a member of an Army air defense artillery unit. In the event of Soviet aerial aggression, I would launch the Nike Hercules missile, a deadly weapon system. Enlisting in the Army was due in large part because of my respect for Dad, who served in World War II.

At the age of 28, Ernest Sandoval Escobedo entered active duty on July 29, 1942, at Fort MacArthur, California. Dad joined thousands of Mexican-American soldiers dedicated to defending the United States. He landed on Normandy beach on D-Day on June 6, 1944, with tens of thousands of other soldiers; it was the epic battle of World War II. Dad was assigned to the 92nd Signal Battalion, Company C, and served as a telephone lineman. He witnessed world history unfolding before his eyes. Dad fought in several ferocious battles and was wounded on April 17, 1945, in Germany. While a patient at William Beaumont General Hospital, in El Paso, Texas, he was discharged from the Army on May 3, 1946. He walked with a limp all his life but never complained of his war injury.

We were all proud of Dad's wartime service. He rarely talked about his combat experiences; I can only imagine that combat had many unspeakable moments. He treasured his olive-green metal footlocker that had functioned as a display case for wartime memorabilia. He used it to store his Army ribbons and decorations. It also contained his discharge papers and Army documents. At times he would look at his Purple Heart medal. I always wondered what his war mementos meant to him; I kept his dog tags, helmet, canteen, and load-bearing belt. He made his transition to civilian life through his proactive approach to life. From him, I learned that you create your opportunities. He never said that I should join the military, but it was an unspoken family expectation.

Mom and Dad were surprised when I indicated that I was entering the military. They were both apprehensive about my decision. Thinking back to his time on active duty, Dad offered me some advice, "Don't let anyone point a weapon at you, and don't let anyone snap you with a towel." Mom wanted me to call her when I got to Fort Bliss. I was confident that I would excel in a military environment.

I arrived in El Paso, Texas, on April 4, 1982, and was transported to the Army reception center. The dry, arid West Texas desert reminded me of home. The first few days were the calm before the storm. After viewing the movie, *The D.I.* (1957), I knew what was in store for recruits. While I was slightly overweight, I looked forward to beginning a metamorphosis into a soldier. Looking at me, the cook, during my first meal in the mess hall, shook his head knowing that I would be experiencing a demanding military indoctrination the following day.

The Army is an encapsulated culture, and life in this organization is inherently stressful. New soldiers must learn to respond quickly to orders. The first day in Logan Heights, an Army training center, was an eye-opener. The senior drill instructor informed us, "You are no longer back on the block smokin' and jokin' with your friends. You are here to do or die." I could not believe my eyes; the senior drill instructor looked just like Dad. His military bearing, his nuanced speech, and his muscular physique were all Dad. Clearly, he was a no-nonsense sergeant, who introduced us to his cadre. In no uncertain terms, he made it clear we would soldier, and his clear expectations motivated us.

On a hot April afternoon, our duffle bags were unloaded on the quadrangle, an asphalt rectangular area where we would learn Army drill and ceremonies. When I was called to pick up my bag, I could not find it. I checked the bags at least four or five times. I went into sheer panic and was on the verge of a mental meltdown. Finally, a drill instructor calmly told me to stop looking for the bag. In a disappointed tone, one of the drill instructors asked everyone to look at their bag to see if someone had picked up my bag by mistake. I was relieved when one of the recruits fessed up to taking my duffle bag.

Standing at attention, I could not help but remember *los Niños Héroes* who fought the U.S. Army during the Mexican American War. General Winfield Scott entered Mexico City with 25,000 troops in 1847.

On September 13th the Mexican cadets defended Chapultepec Castle against an invading American army. Legend has it that one of them wrapped himself up in the Mexican flag and jumped to his death rather than let the flag fall into the enemy's hands. I hoped that I would have the same courage in the battle that these boys demonstrated.

After we were dismissed for the day, one of the drill sergeants approached me and called me to the position of attention. He proceeded to give me a wire brushing for being an undisciplined soldier. I looked him straight in the eye and did not blink; he ordered me to cry. Really? Before entering active duty, I knew that everyone who joins the military is subjected to stress. But this had a novel twist to it and was rather surreal — I would not comply. He asked me why I would not cry; incredulously, I told him Chicanos do not cry. But this experience only made me think of the sacrifices of the valiant men who died on the battlefield. That afternoon, after an exceptionally long day, I could not help but think of Dad and his service during World War II and my classmates who served in Vietnam.

The next day we went to get our military haircuts. All the barbers were *mexicanos* just like me. The barber greeted me like an old friend; in Spanish, he asked me how I wanted my hair cut. Smiling, I responded, *deme un corte suave,* give me a stylish trim. The drill sergeants scowled at me because I had spoken with the barber; I countered that it would have been impolite for me not to answer his question. It took the barber one minute to cut my hair.

We were issued our uniforms and gear. The issued boots were not wide enough; yet mine were stamped with a W for wide. From the moment I tried on the boots, I experienced excruciating pain. The drill sergeants could tell that the boots were hurting my feet and they also felt my pain. From this painful experience, I learned that drill sergeants do have a heart. But with time and use, I was able to adjust to the boots. Later I learned that there were extra wide boots stamped WWW. But how was I to know?

Basic Training is an eight-week endurance program. We got up at four o'clock in the morning to square away the barracks. With the dictum Fit to Fight, we started physical training around 5:00 am. Every week we stood by for barracks and wall locker inspection. Every recruit worked hard to have their uniforms cleaned and pressed. We were implored to keep our lockers locked. If you have seen the movie *Full Metal Jacket* (1987) you can appreciate the displeasure that an unlocked locker can bring. Soldiers with unlocked lockers had their uniforms and clothes and personal items strewn throughout the barracks.

At the end of a rather rigorous training day, I knew that the mess hall would be serving hamburgers and desserts. I noticed a long row of cherry pies. At last, I would be rewarded for my efforts. I selected two hamburgers and two slices of cherry pie. As I was getting ready to eat, the senior drill instructor approached me and told me I could only eat one hamburger and no cherry pie for the rest of the training cycle. I did not have any recourse in the matter. I did not know that my weight would be such a big deal; I was designated a road guard because I was overweight.

Learning the basics of being a soldier was elemental. Standing at attention, we learned the preparatory command given to move the formation of soldiers. The Drill Sergeant shouted, "Forward march." Then he started calling cadence:

Drill Sergeant: "Count cadence, delay cadence, count
cadence, count."

Recruits: "One,"

Drill Sergeant: "Hey soldier,"

Recruits: "Two,"

Drill Sergeant: "Better do your best,"

Recruits: "Three,"

Drill Sergeant: "Before you find yourself,"

Recruits: "Four,"

Drill Sergeant: "In the lean and rest."

This was an evocative message on becoming soldiers. And every day we did our best — lest we found ourselves in the lean and rest, starting position for push-ups.

Every evening at 6:00 p.m. I reported to the orderly room for a medical evaluation. It was a busy office with three or four drill sergeants writing training reports. The drill sergeants' demeanor changed to a friendly one; they weighed me and charted my weight loss. I would sit for half an hour and answer basic questions like how I was feeling, and if I wanted to go home. I always answered that I joined the military to serve my country and looked forward to training. Later I learned that a recruit died in the previous training cycle.

We were asked to purchase green and white baseball shirts to run in. I selected the Spanish pronoun ESE to be imprinted on the training shirt. Almost overnight, I had a new name; the drill sergeants now had a sobriquet for me. But I was always mindful that Dad was the original ESE. When I was asked about my middle initial, I would explain, with a wink, that it stood for *simpático*. Now everyone in the unit knew my name.

Even the battery commander was concerned about my physical condition and was actively involved in my training. I was honored that he supervised my physical training. As a former NCO, he would ensure that I did my push-ups and sit-ups as specified by Army training standards. I assumed that because I was the oldest recruit, he was curious about my presence. The NCOs affectionately called me grandpa; the drill instructors joked that I was older than they. Other NCOs would call me junior. But I took everything in stride.

One morning we were introduced to log drills. Eight or nine soldiers would team up on one rather heavy log weighing about 500 pounds. Listening to a cadence called by a drill sergeant, everyone had to do their part in lifting the log above our heads. We also did curls with the log. If there was ever a time to do your best, this was it. It was obvious who was not doing their part in lifting the log.

We all looked forward to mail call. Mom and Dad sent me letters that reminded me of life in Mackey Camp. I knew that they were happy there. When I wrote, I would ask them about Mexican Canyon. The drill sergeants changed their tone when we received care packages. They gently encouraged us to share our treats. I felt blessed when Mom sent me *empanadas* and *bizcochos*, which I handed out to the men that did not get a care package. The pastries were a little bit of home for us.

The weekly barracks inspections were nerve-racking. I made every effort to adhere to Army Regulation 670-1 Wear and Appearance of Army Uniforms and Insignias. We spent our free time getting ready for the dreaded white glove inspections. The sergeants would open our wall lockers. All the shirt buttons were to be buttoned, and socks carefully rolled. There was a drill instructor who could unbutton a shirt just by reaching in and flicking the button. Of course, he was smiling as he was doing this; then he would ask me why I did not button my shirt.

The Army, for good reason, wants everything to be super clean. In the morning, fine dust from the West Texas desert covered everything. Most recruits just buckled down and cleaned, others just wanted to wish the work away. My thumb even turned green from cleaning the latrine. Each day we cleaned everything — several times.

In recognition of Native American warriors, while circling the quadrangle, we would jog clapping to the chant "Delta on the warpath!" Sounding off at the top of our lungs, the mantra was deafening. We filed into a briefing room still sounding off; then the commander would signal for silence to talk to us about an important training issue. We would exit to the same vocalization. Where do men and women have the freedom of participating in this type of military ritual?

The drill sergeants found a way to infuse a dash of American mythology into our training. Based on the womanizing antihero, Jody is the unapologetic con man who causes untold problems for soldiers. Jody is the guy who never served in the military who stole your car or your girlfriend. Known as Jody Calls, some of these cadences were rather musical:

Drill Sergeant: "Jody this and Jody that."

Recruits: "Your left your right your left."

Drill Sergeant: "Jody was a real cool cat."

Recruits: "Your left your right your left."

Drill Sergeant: "Singing all night."

Recruits: "All night."

Drill Sergeant: "Alright."

Recruits: "Alright."

Drill Sergeant: "Up on your left, oh baby."

Recruits: "Up on your left, oh baby."

The drill sergeants incorporated the Jody specter into cautionary tales related to our military training.

I found it surprising that comedy was part of the military experience. Sometimes life mirrors art. There was the Chicano who convinced the drill sergeants to let him sing cadence to the lyrics of *Doo Wah Diddy Diddy*, just as Bill Murray did in the movie *Stripes* (1981). He was certainly a motivated soldier. One of the officers joked that soldiers were joining the Army to lose weight. I made the sergeants laugh when they gave me a buffer to polish the floors; the machine flew out of control. Much later I learned to operate the buffer with a single hand. And then there was the rowdy recruit who, taking his cue from the movie *Stripes*, banged trash cans together to get everyone up and going in the morning.

At the beginning of May, on a rather hot day, the drill sergeants asked us if we wanted to go swimming. We were sure that there was a covert reason, and we would not enjoy the experience. Disappointed with our silence, the drill sergeants marched us to a sand-filled lot and selected a few recruits to move to the edge of the lot. The recruits were ordered to dive into the sand pool and start swimming. Eventually, I was selected to dive into the sand pool. But because I was not a good swimmer, the drill sergeants yelled, "Save that man; he is drowning." A recruit came to my aid and pushed me across the sandpit. It became clear to me what soldiers were talking about when they discussed chewing some of the same dirt in a combat zone.

I knew that eventually I would be assigned to work in the mess hall. KP duty is a time-honored duty that all soldiers participate in. For some reason, the drill sergeants were thinking of not assigning me this duty. But the soldiers in my unit protested, and I spent a day washing pots and pans in a hot kitchen; I also wiped the walls clean. I wanted to try my hand at cooking; I wanted to prepare *enchiladas* for hungry soldiers. But the mess sergeant was not interested in my cooking. I was happy that the time went fast; one day of this duty was plenty for me.

Just like in the movies, a fight broke out between two soldiers. This could have been a scene from the movie *From Here to Eternity* (1953). Fists were flying with all the troops watching the theatrical spectacle; the drill sergeants thoroughly enjoyed this pugilistic event. The fight lasted a few minutes, then ended quickly. The drill sergeants dubbed one of the fighters Mike Tyson. The next day the senior drill instructor gave his approval to the fighting soldiers saying that is what soldiers do. I came to appreciate hand-to-hand combat as a necessary skill set.

After we were issued our M-16 weapon, one immature recruit decided to point his weapon at me. I was extremely angry with his irresponsible behavior; I scolded the soldier for being so reckless as to point his rifle at a fellow soldier. I had to threaten him with bodily harm to get him to point his weapon away from me. Soldiers being shot by an "unloaded" weapon is legendary. In 1991, U.S. Army General David Petraeus was accidentally shot by a U.S. soldier.

The training sergeants had their sense of humor. On the day we were to receive instruction on the proper handling of a hand grenade, they had all the recruits sit on bleachers. The casual way they were handling a rather lethal explosive device made me wonder how this training session was going to end. So, the sergeant tells his assistant not to drop the hand grenade, and sure enough, he drops it. I thought we were all going to die or be injured. The hand grenade was inert and used for training purposes. The sergeants had their fun, and we lived another day.

I almost did not complete basic training. During the seventh week, I became extremely ill; I went to the troop clinic for medical treatment. The drill sergeant that went with me to the clinic did not let up on me until the doctor confirmed I had contracted strep throat; I had all the symptoms. Swallowing food was painful; I had swollen lymph nodes and was vomiting. I lost any desire to eat the MREs and lost about forty pounds of weight. I had a bad cough that I could not shake. In time I was able to recover and continued to train hard. By the end of basic training, I was in top physical condition.

An Army photographer took a portrait photograph of every soldier after a day of grass drills and low crawling through an obstacle course. Wearing a wrinkled Battle Dress Uniform (BDU), I was dirty and looked like I had been working in the hot West Texas desert. Instead, the Army should have hired a commercial photographer to take a color portrait during the final inspection when soldiers wear their class A uniforms. Every living room in the country has at least one of these military portraitures. For me, the photograph is reminiscent of a special time in my life.

In the morning before we went out to the firing range, in a time-honored tradition, we put on jagged camouflage with a pattern of black, dark green, light green, and brown colors. The guys carefully engaged in an artistic ritual that soldiers have always engaged in, and we were fascinated with the process; we would ask each other to critique the outcome. Arriving at the firing zone, we had our load-bearing belt and our weapons. Our first stop was the gas chamber where we learned to don gas masks quickly. The CS gas consists of a 2-chlorobenzalmalononitrile compound. I was pleased that the experience did not faze me. We were introduced to a wide assortment of weapons. I got a chance to fire the M72 LAW missile. Tossing a hand grenade is an exhilarating experience that causes your heart to pump fast. I was awarded the expert emblem for my efforts.

Firing the M-16 was reminiscent of celebrating the New Year in Mackey Camp. The Drill Instructors were more patient with us as they offered marksmanship pointers. I was interrupted while I was on the firing line and was asked if I was a doctor. I could only think that I had finished a master's degree in 1979. Somewhat irritated, I responded "No." While I was awarded the marksmanship emblem, the qualifying event was rushed and less than satisfactory for me.

We participated in a live-fire exercise at night adjusting our aim using green or red tracers. The exercise was way cool as the green or red tracers found their target downrange. The most dangerous training involved low crawling through a live-fire course. We were instructed not to stand up no matter what happened during live fire. Machine gun rounds whizzed over our heads. One of the live-fire training sergeants threw an aluminum tube at me that landed just inches from me. It looked just like a bomb and for a second, I thought I was going to die in a training accident. But I ignored the *faux* bomb and completed the low crawling exercise. I made a mental note to look up the sergeant after basic. This training was exciting, and what I thought soldiers did this on a daily basis.

To the sound of exploding mortar fire, the 45-mile march back to Logan Heights started at 2:00 a.m. We had an unforgettable experience and were ready to start marching back to Fort Bliss. During the march, the word was that we would be attacked with a chemical weapon; many of us guessed that it would come from an airplane. The battery commander tried to distract us while the drill sergeants ignited CS gas behind us, but we were able to don our gas masks. There were a few soldiers who refused to march back and were transported to Logan Heights by truck; we arrived at 5:00 p.m. in time for dinner. The soldiers who did not participate in the march were forced to stand as we paraded by them.

At the end of basic training, one of the drill instructors suggested that I join the DI cadre. I would have to attend drill sergeant school and endure basic training a second time. While I was honored with the heartfelt invitation, I felt inadequate for the job; you must be an exceptional soldier to be a DI. The drill sergeant was disappointed that I had demurred; I had a tremendous amount of respect for my drill instructors. I was sad to learn that R. Lee Ermey, who gave an Oscar-worthy performance as Gunnery Sergeant Hartman in *Full Metal Jacket* (1987), died on April 15, 2018. The U.S. Army tweeted, "Rest in peace gunny. Semper Fi." By any measure, military life is a demanding and serious business.

I requested to speak to the battery commander on my last day in Logan Heights. This was more of a social visit than anything else; I told the commander that I enjoyed training under his command. He shared with me that he came up the ranks and hoped to see me around Fort Bliss. He also shared his insight into the final barracks inspection and was pleased that I had lost a lot of weight. He said that he might leave the Army to join the FBI.

Leaving for electronics school was a welcomed transition. We were issued seven yellow very thick electronics manuals on the Nike Hercules missile system. Looking at its sleek beautiful design, intuitively you knew it was a formidable weapon system. The black and white missile is 41-feet-long (27-feet-long second stage), weighs 10,710 pounds, with a top speed of 2,778 miles per hour. For six months we spent each day tracing electronic circuits and training on tracking units. We were all told that the missile carried a high explosive warhead; later I learned that the warhead could also be a 30-kiloton nuclear device. The missile system was activated in 1958 with a thirty-year life cycle.

On occasion, we received technical education on electronics and mathematics. One day a young sergeant provided instruction on mathematics; he did not understand the connection between exponents and logarithms. I helped him out with the basic rules. My classmates were impressed with my knowledge of mathematics, and the battery sergeant wanted me promoted on the spot. Knowing a little math is good in any workplace.

In April 1983, *A Nation at Risk: The Imperative for Educational Reform* was released by Terrel H. Bell, Secretary of Education. This report was a clarion call to improve education for students. It warned, "Our Nation is at risk. Our once unchallenged preeminence in commerce, industry, science, and technological innovation is being overtaken by competitors throughout the world. This report is concerned with only one of the many causes and dimensions of the problem, but it is the one that undergirds American prosperity, security, and civility... If an unfriendly foreign power had attempted to impose on America the mediocre educational performance that exists today, we might well have viewed it as an act of war." The report was an indictment of the American educational system. Representing the National Commission on Excellence in Education, David Pierpont Gardner observed, "Our purpose has been to help define the problems afflicting

American education and to provide solutions, not search for scape-goats. We addressed the main issues as we saw them but have not attempted to treat the subordinate matters in any detail." Congress responded to this national issue by pursuing educational reform. I found this report food for thought as I was planning my future.

Army officers are the ruling elite; collectively they are hard-working soldiers who are responsible for meeting military goals. As an enlisted soldier, I could be working on a sophisticated weapon system or mowing the grass depending on the whim of my supervisor; I was not part of the decision-making loop. And from my day-to-day experiences, I was sure that I was not going to become a career soldier. I hoped for career autonomy that was not possible in the Army. I would visualize myself stepping onto Harvard Yard in pursuit of a better life. I set my sights on obtaining a good-paying job that would allow me to purchase a home.

Wednesday morning, October 23, 1983, our commander informed us that the United States barracks in Beirut, Lebanon, had been bombed, and 241 U.S. soldiers had died in the attack. The captain berated us for the soldiers killed in the bombing, stating that if the enlisted soldiers guarding the installation had done their jobs, the tragedy could have been averted. He did not mention that President Ronald Reagan had sent the service members to Beirut as part of a multinational force. In 1985, the Inman Report, prepared by flag officers, stated that Marine officers had failed to protect the soldiers on duty at the time.

I was on active duty at the height of the Cold War. We feared that an unintentional misstep could lead to full-scale war. During a cold night in September 1983, Stanislav Petrov, a Soviet lieutenant colonel, was commanding a Soviet radar site. The radar had wrongly detected five missiles heading for the Soviet Union from bases in the United States. Petrov concluded that the equipment had malfunctioned, and his decision is credited for preventing thermonuclear war. In 2006, the United Nations recognized Petrov as the man who saved humanity.

Again in 1983, NATO launched Able Archer 83, a simulated nuclear war scenario. The war game was so realistic that the Soviet Union was convinced that western countries were planning a preemptive nuclear attack. A Soviet spy was able to provide accurate information to the Kremlin that the actual intent of headquarter command in Belgium was not to start a nuclear war. The world again came close to nuclear Armageddon during this military exercise.

With the roll-out of the Patriot missile, I witnessed the evolution of Army missile systems. After a year of tracing the intricate circuits of the Nike Hercules radar system, we transitioned to a new generation missile system. The Patriot missile system functions as a mobile weapon that can quickly be moved in half an hour. Encased in a rectangular frame, four missiles are ready to be fired, with each missile being 19 feet long and weighing 1,500 pounds having a launch velocity of Mach 4.1.

I spent about a year maintaining the Patriot missile system at White Sands Missile Range, in New Mexico, and tracked jets flying out of Holloman Air Force Base located near Alamogordo. Every day we would run system diagnostics and obtain a BRU list to find hardware faults in the missile system. The Patriot missile is a solid-state system, while the Nike Hercules system electronics consisted of vacuum tubes and metal relays.

The Soviet military went on full alert on October 14, 1984. NBC anchor Tom Brokaw reported that the Soviet Far East Army was ready to go to war. The Kremlin condemned President Ronald Reagan for joking about bombing Russia. The President did not realize how close the United States and the Soviet Union came to an unintended nuclear war. I did not want to contemplate a nuclear doomsday due to a human error; I was thankful for the restraint of two rival nations.

It seemed that Harvard professors were always making the news. Harvard professor Sara Lawrence-Lightfoot authored the award-winning study *The Good High School: Portraits of Character and Culture* in 1983. This study examined six high schools. Professor Lightfoot used portraiture, a metaphor, to describe her research methodology. For my Harvard dissertation, I thought of conducting an ethnographic study of the El Paso schools.

My battery sergeant approached me about attending nuclear, biological, and chemical warfare training. He knew that I did not want this assignment. But who did? This was a dangerous and highly specialized job. For the first time, I was taking coursework with officers and senior NCOs. We were introduced to the devastating effects of nerve and blood agents. We continued by studying the destructive effects of an EMP pulse if a nuclear war were to take place. Our job was to perform paper and pencil calculations on radiation exposure using a nomograph. The course lasted three weeks, and I was glad when it ended. American citizens are aware of nerve agents and biological attacks but have limited information on the threat to the national electrical grid.

Eventually, I was considered for promotion to sergeant and was to be interviewed by my first sergeant. As a former drill instructor, he was a lean, tough supervisor. His first question centered on why I joined the Army. I told him that I joined the military as a matter of family tradition and patriotism. He dismissed my answer and said I joined because of economic reasons, which is true of many Chicanos who join the military. But not in my case. I could only guess that he was projecting his reasons for joining the Army.

In time, I became a systems maintenance sergeant for the Logistics Readiness Center. I worked as a liaison between the Patriot units, Patriot Project Office, Raytheon, and Herc-Patriot Maintenance Division. I gathered and analyzed information on the readiness of Patriot battalions by publishing Patriot Status Reports, which were submitted to the Brigade Commander.

Every noncommissioned officer undergoes an evaluative process as mandated by AR 623-205. I worked extremely hard at my assigned tasks. I was pleased with my review, which stated: "SGT Escobedo is the consummate soldier. A top performer in the area of computer technology, he has demonstrated exceptional ability in database management and associated administrative responsibilities. His leadership attributes, specifically his ability to initiate and execute assigned projects, makes him an indispensable asset. His knowledge of the Patriot missile weapon system and technical and tactical proficiency has resulted in the certification and deployment of combat-ready Patriot battalions. Additionally, he has demonstrated ability to communicate and interact effectively with senior officers and subordinates. SGT Escobedo has performed all his duties in a conscientious and impeccable manner." I did my part as a soldier to defend the nation.

I requested my commander that I be allowed to attend a college class to study statistics. I explained that this course would make me a more productive soldier who was charged with data collection and analysis. The professor who taught the course and I became good friends; her iridescent personality motivated the class to learn the subject content. She listened to my career dreams with quiet skepticism; although I finished the course with an A, she said that I would never be admitted to Harvard. I had to find out for myself if this was true.

As a sergeant, I was entitled to a single occupancy room. The furniture was old and worn but reminded me of my *abuelita's* furniture. I tried to keep my room inspection ready so the battery sergeant would not complain. After duty hours I would read a wide range of books dealing with military matters. I read *The Art of War* by Sun Tzu (written between 475 and 221 B.C.E.), *On War* (1832) by Carl von Clausewitz, and *On Thermonuclear* War (1960) by Herman Kahn. These books gave purpose to my day-to-day work of maintaining a missile system.

I dreamed that I led soldiers in PT, physical training, under the watchful eye of an Army captain. Starting with a rhythmic clap during the 3-mile run, I would sing cadence to modified lyrics of *Land of a Thousand Dances,* a classic rock and roll song and favorite among Chicanos. Obviously, I did not have the voice of Frankie Garcia, the lead singer for Cannibal and the Headhunters, the legendary Chicano band. *Raza* in the unit liked it, but the white soldiers were indifferent. The black soldiers were okay with this cadence. At the end of the morning run, I ordered the soldiers to fall out. The captain wanted the soldiers to perform cool-down exercises and had me call them back. So, we performed the mountain climber exercise. What a memorable reverie.

I knew the day would come when I would have a showdown with the Marines who were training at Fort Bliss. In the evenings I would jog at the track for half an hour. On a perfect October afternoon, I ran by two young soldiers wearing gold and red Marine colors. They could not have been older than 18 years old. No words were exchanged; I picked up my pace and so did the Marines. I laid down the challenge. We were competing in a race to determine if the Army or Marines were better. While I gave 100 percent, I lost the race to the Marines. Next time it would be a different outcome. Every November 10th on Marine Corps Day, I fondly remember the two young Marines.

Physical training is a way of life on all military installations. On one occasion I was selected to carry the Commandant's flag on a post-run; this was an honor given to outstanding soldiers. This meant that I would run with the Commandant and the brigade colonel. After 45 minutes my strength began to wane; the last thing I wanted was to do was drop the general's flag. At the end of the run, he gave me a badge depicting a running soldier carrying a red flag imprinted with a single silver star. I thanked him for the memento and went my way.

The Army is a uniquely different type of organization. I was surprised when a good friend with the rank of Sergeant First Class casually said that he would be honored to take a bullet for me in combat. I could only respond to him that he was an exceptional soldier and hoped that he would never find himself fighting on a battlefield. We had a special bond that explained his heartfelt pledge. This vignette impressed upon me that soldiers have an existential purpose in life; we will fight to protect soldiers in harm's way.

One morning, after PT, an Army recruiter approached me to join the 82nd Airborne Division and said that this military unit called Fort Bragg home. He told me the 82nd Airborne Division had a distinguished combat history. I thanked him for the invitation and commented that I was too old to be jumping out of C-130s. I advised him that I had good reason not to take him up on his offer; I was approaching my Expiration Term of Service and planned to attend graduate school.

Even when I wore the uniform, I hoped to teach at a college. There was a job announcement in the *El Paso Times* seeking a math instructor to teach technical math to electricians. I was fortunate enough to get a teaching job at the local college. For some reason, the manager of business and industry was not in agreement with me being hired. I was surprised because I had both a math degree and a master's degree in hand. I guess it was not enough that I was working on a sophisticated missile system as my day job. All the students were *raza*. The course went well with one of the electricians wanting to hire me just to do math calculations for him. This was my first job as a college instructor and laid the foundation for becoming a full-time college teacher.

El Paso is an extraordinary city for soldiers to be stationed in. The *mexicanos* call the city *El Chuco* because it is the home of *pachuquismo*. The first Pachuco I met had an imperceptible swagger; he wore a turquoise shirt and pressed blue jeans. He was intelligent and well-spoken. His black shoes had metal taps and made a clicking sound when he walked. He was in control of his social environment and was intensely interested in cars.

With its colleges and universities, restaurants, museums, libraries, and theatrical productions, El Paso has a lot to offer. I liked the small Mexican bars and grills where trios play anything you wanted to hear; I usually requested *boleros*. All the *trios* performed *Mil Besos*, a traditional Mexican standard. One afternoon, walking down Montana Avenue, I was stopped by a muscular Chicano wearing sunglasses and a tee-shirt; he asked me for a dollar. Unexpectedly, after I gave him the dollar, he recited an original poem for me. To this day I wish I had a copy of his poem about *raza* identity in a border community. I was impressed with his introspection into life, and we became good friends.

José grew up in *el segundo barrio*, where many Mexicans stopped on their initial entry into the United States. To him, cultural identity was central to his persona. When he was not with his *hyna*, that is his girlfriend, he would invite me to Rafa's Bar and Grill where he would tell me about his various life challenges and changing *barrio* landscape. I could not help but think how interesting his life was; he had a natural optimism for life. On some days we would go to the Hollywood Cafe, located in midtown, and enjoy lunch.

I had the privilege of meeting his uncle, who had lived in El Paso all his life. Located south of I-10, his home reminded me of Mexican Canyon; his home was comfortable and had a painting of the *Virgen de Guadalupe* with votive candles burning in the living room. He had a genial way of talking. After greeting me, he paused momentarily to size me up and said that I would accomplish a lot in life. After all, he had experienced life and had a sense of the future. I came to learn that he served in the Army; he shared his Korean battlefield experiences and how machine gun fire had ripped holes in his leg. Working as a security guard, he has managed to move forward in life on his terms.

Stopping at a Circle K to buy a soft drink, I saw some young Chicanos hanging out outside the store. One of them was wearing a Class A Army uniform; he looked sharp. Following in the tradition of many *raza*, he was ready to serve in the military. The uniform was clean and the shoes new, but he was not a soldier. The shoes were not polished, his haircut did not adhere to Army standards, and his uniform lacked insignias, military ribbons, and medals. I hoped that a family member would give him sound advice about entering military service. I could only assume that he would join the Army in a year or so.

One afternoon, as I was sitting in the Lariat, an El Paso café, my former senior drill instructor walked up and greeted me. He was attired in a fine West Texas cowboy dress. I remembered that one of the drill sergeants told us not to bother him if we saw him in a restaurant. I was pleased that the senior drill instructor did not share the same viewpoint. I always admired him for being fair-minded in dealing with new soldiers. He asked how my work was going in my air defense unit. I invited him to join me at my table, and we reminisced about our soldiering experiences.

Toward the end of my tour, I applied for a White House Fellowship. This program was established by President Johnson in 1962. Highly competitive by design, I knew that my chances of being selected were remote; I wanted the experience of shaping national public policy. Part of the application included writing a policy memo. My commander was gracious enough to endorse my application. Later I learned that military officers have the inside track, and consequently I was not selected.

A few months before my separation from the Army, I applied for a job as a university registrar. Going into the hiring process, I realized that internal candidates have the inside track. I felt I had strong credentials and job experience for the position. Twenty university administrators and faculty members interviewed me. I was asked rather complex questions about the operation of a registration office. While I did not receive a job offer, the experience opened my eyes to the importance of academic credentials. I wondered if I had had a Harvard degree in hand if it would have made a difference.

As a 37-year-old I had to select a career. The Army offered me nearly $25,000 to reenlist. My commander wanted me to attend Officer Candidate School, but my mind was set on attending Harvard.

The clock was ticking, and I could not afford to waste precious time. I planned to use my Veteran Educational Assistance Program benefits to defray some of the cost. Equally important, I was eligible for a Veterans Administration loan to buy a home.

Dad wrote me an encouraging letter toward the end of my time in the Army:

January 20, 1986

Miami Arizona

Dear Son,

Just a few lines to say hi to you. Am sure glad you wrote. Obviously, you are in the best of health — that is what doing pushups do for you. According to your plans, you have decided to leave the Army. You say you liked the service. I believe if I were you, I would stay in the service for 20 years. Time has a way of rushing by. Serve your 20 years and then see in which direction you are going. In my book, you are doing fine regardless. Son, you will do just fine either way you go. You have made the right decision. See you soon. Your Pa who thinks of you all the time.

Always,

ESE

Dad's letter made a lot of sense; it made me think about the benefits of staying in the Army. Yet I had to be true to my belief that I could succeed in academia.

My last day on active duty, before going on terminal leave, was memorable. My commander gave me a Patriot lapel pin. I was relieved that I was not leaving with any service-connected injuries. I went over to the administrative offices to pick up my DD 214. I was given an honorable discharge. In block 13 for decorations, I was recognized for Rifle M16-marksmanship, hand grenade-expert, Army Service Ribbon, Good Conduct Medal, and Army Commendation Medal. My separation code was LBK and my reenlistment code was RE-1. I left my unit on good terms knowing that some soldiers would continue my duties.

Before leaving El Paso, I bought Dad a light blue baseball cap that had ARMY embroidered in red lettering. When I handed him the cap, I could tell that it brought back fond memories; he wore it all the time. He asked me what it was like to launch a Nike Hercules missile; I told him it was a spectacular event. It was important to me to have made a small contribution to national defense.

I felt that I had made a positive contribution to the U.S. Army and requested a letter of recommendation. The letter dated September 1, 1989, stated: "This letter is to certify that Mr. Ernest G. Escobedo worked in the area of computer technology. While he was assigned at this brigade his computer work involved installing IBM PCs, implementing its programming, and facilitating and developing functional software. Additional duties involved training officers and staff in the use of these computers and developing an automation plan that was established as a brigade standard. For these accomplishments in computer automation, he was awarded the Army Commendation Medal on March 31, 1985."

Four years of active duty went by fast. Years later, I would drive from Phoenix to El Paso to tour Logan Heights; this Army training site has long been leveled. You have so many memories when you leave a military unit. I admired the drill sergeants who had little time to transform us into soldiers. Not a day goes by that I do not reflect on my time at Fort Bliss. I only regret not signing up for an airborne unit. I felt humbled that I was allowed to work on Nike Hercules and Patriot missile systems, and pleased to contribute a technology plan to the Army.

Passed on November 6, 1986, the Immigration Reform and Control Act (IRCA) would impact the lives of *mexicanos* struggling to make a living. The law stipulated that U.S. employers would be fined if they hired undocumented workers. The intent of this legislation was to stop immigration and to crush the Mexican community economically. Historically, they have performed the most labor-intensive and dangerous work in the nation. Inevitably, I anticipated that *raza* civil rights would be abused and many would lose their jobs. Nevertheless, Chicano comedians admired the work ethic of *raza*, a sentiment that resonated with their audiences. Undocumented workers would continue to participate in the underground economy and toil at the lowest paying wages.

After completing my active-duty commitment, I felt that a computer science degree would help me stay current in a changing world. On the eleventh of August 1988, I completed a Computer Science degree with honors from Pima College; my technical training was obsolete almost immediately. I had reached a life-defining inflection point. I was ready to move forward to continue my journey toward realizing my dream; I was ready to start my doctoral program at Harvard.

"The [social policy] class [that I taught] was important as it provided a focal point for Harvard students to critically examine issues around language and immigration. The vivid, fruitful, and satisfying images that I have of my Harvard experience was the informal policy-related conversations I had with the ten to fifteen Hispanic students after class."

— Raul Yzaguirre, Harvard Professor, NCLR CEO, October 1, 1997

5

HARVARD LIFE

REAMS CAN COME TRUE. I received my Harvard admissions letter dated April 8, 1987. Growing up in Mexican Canyon with limited academic and financial resources, I intuitively knew that I would be tested in many ways to adjust to life in Cambridge. Destiny was offering me a world-class education that would open doors of opportunity for me. Mom and Dad were surprised that I had been accepted to an elite university. Yet, they were not certain how I would pay for private education. I had no idea if I could perform the daunting academic work that laid before me. I calculated the opportunity costs and decided that the benefits were greater than the financial risks.

It almost seems like yesterday that Hector Avalos was encouraging me to attend Harvard University. He provided me a panoramic view of life at Harvard. A *colega* from Tucson, he was enrolled in the Graduate School of Arts and Sciences, and it almost seemed like a foregone conclusion to him that I would be admitted to this venerable institution. But I had my doubts. I have always appreciated his generous and optimistic encouragement about pursuing the doctorate. I found his Harvard dissertation *Illness and Health Care in the Ancient Near East: The Role of the Temple in Greece, Mesopotamia, and Israel* (1991) to be a masterful account of biblical times.

Admissions committees place a lot of importance on the applicant's statement of purpose. My application for admission to Harvard was based on the premise that the pursuit of excellence should be the singular standard for study at the graduate level. I was upfront that I came from low socioeconomic status; I did not know if I would fit in with students from the upper class. Since my formative years, I have had a sense of the strong influence of socioeconomic status and cultural capital needed to succeed in life. I cited my background in mathematics, military service, participation in public service, earning a graduate degree, and working as a computer programmer as a good reason to be admitted to Harvard. Attending Harvard, I argued, would change my career trajectory, and advance my participation in public service. Moreover, I wished to develop expertise in social policy. I hoped to become a college professor and eventually a college dean. Colleges need Latino educators who have an intrinsic understanding of Latino students' culture, language, and aspirations. I noted that institutional values should be based on the precepts of an egalitarian society. I included my hope to be active in promoting equity and inclusion in public institutions. I shared what my research agenda would look like at Harvard. I concluded by stating that public policy formation is not a spectator sport but required people to advocate for the public interest.

I wondered how Harvard would change my life. In a reoccurring dream, I found the answer. Straight out of a Wizard of Oz-like reverie, I had a technicolor experience walking along Brattle Street, the main boulevard in Cambridge. The edge of the sidewalk was carpeted with a rainbow of flowers. I could hear Ersi Arvizu's song *Sabor a mí* coming from a distant tavern. A small, obscure black and white sign pointed the way to Byerly Hall, the Harvard admissions office. Undergraduates were discussing the momentous issues of the day, professors sat in cafes discussing the arts and humanities, Kennedy School students were planning political campaigns, business students strategized how to leverage international monetary policy, and philosophers discussed the ontological aspects of life. The Harvard bookstore advertised its latest best-seller *Mexican Canyon*. Life was perfect. Waking up from this Elysium dream, made me pause to reflect on my blessings.

A mythical university among institutions of higher learning, Harvard admits students from many countries, and competition is intense for a handful of spaces. Every year about 20,000 students attend classes at Harvard. The university is an academic megapolis of an undergraduate college, graduate, and professional schools located at different places. Latinos represent 12 percent of admitted students to Harvard College. I was admitted to a doctoral program for full-time study, and the Committee on Degrees (COD) would review my doctoral research. I selected coursework that would make me competitive for employment at any university or college.

Admissions to Ivy League schools have been shaped by evolving affirmative action law. Nine years had passed since the U.S. Supreme Court issued a ruling on affirmative action in *Regents of the University of California v. Bakke*. Allan Bakke sued the University of California Davis School of Medicine over its admissions policies. In 1978 the U.S. Supreme Court in a 5-4 decision ruled that colleges and universities could not use racial quotas as part of their admissions criteria. Harvard University had submitted an *amicus* brief indicating that socioeconomic factors were relevant to the admissions process.

Everyone in the family was happy that I would be studying at the premier university in the world. The late Dr. Rogelio Reyes would have been supportive of my interest in establishing the Mexican Canyon Harvard Club. My undergraduate work was a starting point where I would develop an appreciation for academia. My graduate work must have had a Pygmalion effect on me; I became more confident about my ability to succeed in an academic setting. Family members would casually mention to friends and neighbors that I would be studying at Harvard; this would become a source of family pride. My classmates would be the sons and daughters of CEOs and presidents from around the world.

I am mindful of other Chicanos who came before me who ventured into the Harvard strata. In his memoir, Enrique Hank Lopez described how his family moved from Bachimba, Chihuahua, to El Paso and then to Denver. He described the feeling of being an uprooted *mexicano*. Certainly, I would have liked to talk to him about his undergraduate years and subsequent quest to earn a Harvard Law School degree. He was a highly respected attorney who wrote about the Harvard mindset. However, the *Harvard Crimson* eviscerated his book *The Harvard Mystic* (1979), intimating that it lacked substance. Yet, he returned to Harvard to teach at the Kennedy School. I envisioned similar scenarios that would cast doubt on my qualifications to write an ethnography on life at Harvard.

My address for the next two years would be Six Ash Street, Cambridge, Massachusetts 02138. It was not until many years later that I realized how exclusive this zip code was. While the New

England architecture had a certain elegance, moving to Cambridge was a source of stress; I was aware that living in a cosmopolitan area was expensive. Yet, I was looking forward to a rare excursion to the North End with all its fabulous Italian restaurants. I was lucky that Harvard offered graduate housing close to campus; I would not need a car to commute to campus. I did not have to think twice about this decision and signed a housing contract to live in Cambridge.

My flight arrived late in the evening at Logan Airport. A friendly Jamaican cabbie loaded my bags and we proceeded onto Storrow Drive and then onto Memorial Drive. Taking a turn onto Hawthorn Street, he was able to take me to the Cronkhite Graduate Center on Ash Street. Exhausted from the plane ride, I walked into the lobby and was greeted by a *Chilango* — a resident from Mexico City. He probably was from the *Lomas de Chapultepec* where the upper-class live. He was excited to be studying at Harvard with other *mexicanos*. Later I came to understand that I was not a true Mexican in his eyes, and he quickly lost his enthusiasm for forming a friendship with me. After he graduated from the Kennedy School, he started working for the McKinsey Group, an international management consulting firm.

It was a five-minute walk from Cronkhite to Longfellow Hall, home of the administrative offices of the Harvard Graduate School of Education, where I would pursue my doctorate. During the admissions orientation, we were told that it was not necessary to tiptoe past the admissions office – we were in. We listened to a presentation on the School and its impressive resources. The classrooms and library are equally close to the graduate center. Later we would meet the faculty.

Harvard professors' academic brilliance was obvious; I felt blessed to study under the tutelage of national policy scholars and admired them for their expansive intellectual background. Harvard hires professors who publish extensively in their field and are deemed to possess the scholarly and social attributes needed to teach at a top-tier university. There was a MacArthur scholar who was a sociologist; she graduated from Harvard College and had an enviable track record of research. My professors were top-tier academicians with national reputations; many of them worked with federal policymakers on crafting education policy. Some of them were editors of research journals; others served as consultants to international education ministries. The professors were friendly but socially distant. Their priority was conducting research or consulting on global matters. I was open to their ideas, hoping that I could tap this knowledge after leaving Harvard. My goal was to flourish in this demanding academic environment.

I was ambivalent about meeting the members of the doctoral cohort. About 40 very qualified persons would pursue the doctorate along with me. I was the only Chicano in the doctoral cohort. About half of my classmates came from New England; they were all bright and articulate. Due to a wide range of individual backgrounds, I expected some cultural dissonance. But I was attending Harvard to move forward in life and not get bogged down with counterproductive conversations. After the meeting, a Canadian asked me if I knew who the Chicanos were; I was pleased to introduce myself as a Chicano who came from Arizona and that most of Chicanos lived in the Southwest. I felt lucky that I was one of the few *raza* to attend Harvard. The pressure to succeed was a daily preoccupation.

The first two weeks it rained every day. To relieve my anxiety, I would visualize the clear azure blue skies of Arizona. Finally, I could not take the rain anymore; I was planning to return home. A break in the weather gave me a reason to continue my education in Cambridge. Meeting students from around the world, I could only guess that they were from privileged backgrounds. Most of us understood that we had one chance to succeed; we were all busy with heavy academic loads. There was little time to socialize and we dedicated our time to studying; the lights never went out at Cronkhite.

To my surprise, one of the Cronkhite residents asked me if I was a gang member. I could not help but wonder why he would insult me with such rudeness. He did not know that I was a veteran and I had completed a graduate degree. He probably was comparing me to Jose Luis Razo Jr. who was admitted to Harvard in 1985. The national media referred to him as a "the Harvard homeboy" after being arrested for several robberies in California while taking a break from Harvard. Razo probably was culturally alienated and needed a touch of home. Like the rest of us, he needed friends who would give him hope while studying at Harvard. Certainly, he did not take advantage of counseling and mental health services at Harvard. I hoped that I never would have his disaffection with Harvard.

During the shopping week of prospective classes, I expected to enroll in Nathan Glazer's course on social policy. He was a white-haired sociology professor with expertise in policy studies; during his distinguished academic career, he examined race and ethnicity in American society. His book *Beyond the Melting Pot* (1963) was influential in the halls of the federal government during the 1960s. To my surprise, he penned *Affirmative Discrimination* (1975), which was a critique of affirmative action. Later in a New Republic article, *In Defense of Preferences*, he reversed his views on affirmative action. *We Are All Multiculturalists Now* (1997) pointed out that assimilation is not embraced by Chicanos and other cultural groups. Yet, I was overwhelmed by the required core courses and decided against taking his class. On January 19, 2019, Nathan Glazer died at the age of 95 at his home in Cambridge.

As a high school student, I wondered what it would be like to attend a private eastern school. I never imagined that I would have the good fortune to meet the students and faculty of Phillips Exeter Academy, located in New Hampshire. This private school has produced some of the nation's influential people. Andrew Yang, a presidential candidate, graduated from Phillips Exeter in 1992. Christopher Jencks, Harvard social policy theorist, graduated from Phillips Exeter in 1954.

I visited Phillips Exeter in October 1988. Its preeminent faculty and stately campus have a lofty status among private eastern schools. This upper-class school has a ubiquitous aura of privilege. With an endowment of $1.25 billion, this private academy has unparalleled financial resources. Truly a national treasure, students come from around the world to enroll in this academy to receive a first-class education that inevitably leads to admission to Harvard College.

Stepping onto the Phillips Exeter campus, I found my way to the church. Originally a Second Congregational Church built in 1895, the place offers interfaith worship on Wednesdays to students. The polished oak beams and beautifully stained glass provide a majestic setting for fellowship. The school community waited for Patrick O'Donnell to lead the students in meditation. He gave an inspirational message that resonated with the students; he encouraged them to strive for a productive life.

Principal Kendra Stearns O'Donnell was the CEO at the time of my visit. Earning her Ph.D. in English, she had an academic's view and served as the leader of the faculty. Formerly an all-boys preparatory school, she believed in change that is inclusive of all students. A seasoned administrator, she was comfortable wielding power. She was mindful of how her tenure would affect the community of Exonians, students who attend the academy.

At the center of academics at Phillips Exeter is the Harkness table, a Socratic symbol, which is emblematic of high-performance learning. Critical thinking is stressed as central to learning. Students can take a wide range of courses in the humanities, social sciences, languages, mathematics, and sciences. I observed a faculty member providing instruction to students. I was impressed with the students' commitment to learning; later the students engaged in conversations about the course content.

I learned that Phillips Exeter reaches out to underrepresented students and provides scholarships to students with potential. The academy promotes a respectful attitude of all and discourages elitist viewpoints. I hope that my *sobrino* who lives in Globe, Arizona considers studying at this stellar school. Maybe someone from Mexican Canyon would also consider studying at Phillips Exeter. If I had known of the wonderful learning opportunities at this academy, I would have applied for admission to this private school. Certainly, I would have missed Mom and Dad, but I would have had better academic preparation for college.

The capstone experience for Phillips Exeter seniors is the Washington Intern Program that provides a look at the interworking of the power elite. The Exonians listen to senators debate public policy. Students spend a day with a senator where they learn the prerequisites of how to manage the reins of power. After returning to campus, I wondered if my studies at Harvard would lead to a professional position in Washington.

Walking down the hallway of Cronkhite, you would hear government students reciting President John F. Kennedy's 1961 inaugural address, "... Let the word go forth from this time and place, to friend and foe alike, that the torch has been passed to a new generation of Americans — born in this century, tempered by war, disciplined by a hard and bitter peace, proud of our ancient heritage — and unwilling to witness or permit the slow undoing of those human rights to which this Nation has always been committed, and to which we are committed today at home and around the world." They were preparing to assume positions of power at the highest levels of government.

As the days went by, I settled into a predictable routine. I selected an off to the side table in the Cronkhite dining area; in time it acquired an eponymous status. This was where I chose to enjoy an hour of dining and conversation with the Harvard denizens. Sometimes *raza* or a foreign student would join me for dinner. Occasionally, the Kennedy School students would join me for acerbic political debate. They quipped that I spoke in a sesquipedalian, or polysyllabic language. I enjoyed taunting them by saying that Russian tanks would probably be rumbling up Pennsylvania Avenue when they started governing the country.

Inevitably, our conversations would lead to discussing the women of Cronkhite. Some of the men at my table felt intimidated by their natural intelligence and beauty. I pointed out to them that the ladies saw them as the *crème de la crème* who eventually would become professors, lawyers, national political figures, or corporate CEOs. I would encourage them to cross the dining room and invite one of them to share an ice cream dessert to initiate a social conversation. Yet, I never crossed the dining room. My only interest was earning a degree; I could not afford the distraction of beginning a romantic relationship.

Just like Henry Cisneros before them, I admired the few *raza* Kennedy School students. They came from California, Colorado, Arizona, New Mexico, Texas and studied in a two-year master's program that would prepare them to work in Washington or pursue a political career in their communities. Later I learned that one of my *colegas* ascended to the rank of Army general. They invited me to join them at the Institute of Politics to participate in a seminar on Latino social policy.

While not on my transcript, the seminar on immigration and civil rights was an important class I had taken at Harvard. I was impressed with the confidence, competency, and polished lecturing style of Professor Raul Yzaguirre. Only at Harvard could I attend a social policy class taught by a national Chicano leader. We were all in awe of his years working in Washington D.C. on behalf of Latinos. He is a prodigy of governmental processes; I viewed him as the *padrino* of Hispanic America. I was saddened when I could not accept Raul Yzaguirre's invitation to join the National Council of the Raza based in Washington D.C.; I knew that I disappointed him. My family was expecting me to return home, and I would be leaving Harvard with an enormous debt.

The active-duty soldiers who attended the Kennedy School did not have anything to prove. They were serious students, watched their words carefully and were very tolerant of their younger and brash classmates. They encouraged me to return to active duty. One of them spent his weekends flying military jets. These battle-tested warriors were on the fast track to becoming generals.

One Kennedy School student casually mentioned that he was taking an investment course at the Harvard Business School. He intimated that his stock simulation had spiked. I did not realize at the time that maybe I should have also cross-registered at the Harvard Business School and learn about financial investments. I did not know how to buy stocks that would yield a comfortable retirement. I should have said, "Hmmm, tell me more about your investment class." Now I wonder which artificial intelligence stock is being endorsed at the Business School.

One November evening I was filled with anticipation walking to Cronkhite along Brattle Street. Looking through the windows, I would see residents enjoying dinner, usually, chicken or pasta was served. No longer an outsider, I knew that I would be joining them in a few minutes. A recent Harvard College graduate and her friends joined me for dinner. After a few minutes of pleasant conversation, she pointedly asked me if I thought I could write the dissertation. That was the 64-thousand-dollar question. I was surprised and taken aback by the question as much as my professors never raised that point with me.

Former President Barack Obama and I were admitted to Harvard University in the same year. While I never had a personal conversation with the future POTUS, he was a student to be admired. As President, he was committed to immigration reform within the parameters of immigration law. If he had grown up on the border, he would have recognized that Mexicans are not a threat, but neighbors who wish to move freely between two nations. Both of his parents were professors, which gave him a scholarly perspective on life. Some critics insist that he was not a U.S. citizen, underscoring the mentality of the extreme right. Growing up in Indonesia and Hawaii, President Obama has a global view of life. I admired how he crafted his educational experiences, which served him well in his presidency. I hope to meet him someday.

I felt a bond with the black scholars who lived at Cronkhite. They came from across the nation and some were international students.

During the dinner hour, they would discuss their research agendas. They spoke of their professional dreams in academia or corporate America. Unspoken but there, not far from our minds, was the issue of class, race, gender, and ethnicity in the nation. I valued their encouragement as we negotiated our research projects.

I spent my downtime relaxing in Cronkhite's TV room. It was a public area where residents could collect their thoughts. On one occasion a resident from the South, who displayed a confederate battle flag in his room, cornered me on the topic of race. He was very friendly and wanted to discuss all the shortcomings of blacks; for the first time at Harvard, I saw the ugly face of white supremacy. I could only wonder what negative remarks he would make about Mexicans. After listening for a short time, I informed him that I had many black friends, and it was inappropriate to talk about them in a defamatory manner.

Yes, some Southern gentlemen extended their friendship. They were mindful of cultural differences between us; I was appreciative that they were supportive of my educational goals. A good friend from Alabama gave me superb advice on how to finish the dissertation. I knew that they would assume leadership roles in their communities after graduation.

Harvard Square is within a stone's throw from Harvard Yard and has countless shops, office buildings, and numerous cars and pedestrians. On any given day, throngs of people congregate in Harvard Square. A source of a lot of traffic noise, trucks rumble by, new and old cars inch their way down the street. Occasionally a policeman would glance at the traffic. The traffic continued into the intersection even when the pedestrians saw the walk signal light. At the don't walk sign, people ignored it and crossed the street not worrying about traffic. Holding up their hand, gauging the speed of traffic, longtime Cambridge residents walked into oncoming traffic, crossing the intersection with no problem.

Draped in Ivy, Harvard is unlike public universities. Students are eager to share that wine is served at social functions. The deans speak to the autonomous nature of the various schools, with each academic unit being financially responsible within the dictum, every tub on its bottom. In ancient Rome, Appian Way was the grand entrance to the city. At Harvard, the Appian Way is a small obscure street. Even the elevators have a name. One elevator had a tongue-in-cheek name Godot, a character from a Samuel Becket play who never arrives.

Paying for a Harvard education was a daunting realization for me. This was an investment in my future, which I gladly accepted. You must have faith that education is the best investment you can make. I chose to ignore the tuition cost of attending graduate school at a private university. I signed away my financial future by borrowing tons of money. I was in my room at Cronkhite when I opened my first term bill. I almost fainted; I should have been sitting down. The tuition was $11,440 for the academic year. Room and board cost $15,450 for the academic year. I could not believe that room and board could be so expensive. The first year I borrowed $22,215 from Harvard. In the second year, I borrowed the same amount of money.

I was lucky to get a job working in the admissions office. A nascent Harvard experience, I was extremely tired after studying all night, but I would make it to work every morning. I spent my time at work assembling admissions packages and answering inquiries about Harvard. The admission officers worked extremely hard to follow the internal administrative policies. Every effort was made to ensure a level playing field for all applicants. I still possess a two-dollar check from Harvard University dated April 17, 1989, for my work in the admissions office.

I enjoyed interacting with the Harvard professional staff. They had strong interpersonal skills and always had a kind word. They were always ready to help me resolve any organizational hurdle. The managers were all business; they had a lot of responsibility in managing their respective departments. I never complained about the endless regulations, and always was cordial when dealing with Harvard employees.

I happened to meet Lauro F. Cavazos at the Cronkhite Center in October 1989. Appointed by President Ronald Reagan in 1988, he was the first Latino Secretary of Education. He attended Texas Tech as a student, taught there as an anatomy professor, and finally served as president of the university. Later he served as president of Tufts University. A member of the President's domestic council, Cavazos was conducting a series of public hearings around the country on NCLR's education initiative. I was leaving for class, and Cavazos was arriving for a meeting. I greeted him by noting that I did not run into many *Tejanos* in Cambridge. Genuinely interested, he asked me what I was studying. When I told him that I was taking social policy classes, he gave me his business card and asked me to call him. I never called him as I struggled to meet my academic obligations.

Teaching evaluations of Harvard professors were kept in Gutman Library. I was surprised that blistering narratives of a world-class faculty were available for anyone to read. I wondered how any student could sign up for their classes after reading such highly negative reviews. These professors had the power to make you or break you. I made a point never to write an evaluation review of a Harvard professor.

To my surprise, Harvard awards a master's degree in passing to doctoral students. I called Mom and Dad with the good news. They were both happy about this family milestone. Mom told me that Dad was in poor health and that he might not be able to attend commencement festivities. I was concerned because he had been a physically vigorous man all his life. I had a flashback to the days we worked together in Mexican Canyon as he chiseled away at the caliche walls. I was happy that Mom traveled to Cambridge to see me graduate from Harvard University.

I received my master's degree from Harvard on June 8th, 1989. The Harvard graduates were greeted by pleasant spring rain, yet the happiness and joy of graduating students cannot be diminished by a spring shower. We walked from Cronkhite to the Yard where families sat waiting for the graduation exercises to begin. I told Mom that the diploma belonged to her as well. Harvard diplomas have two dates — the date the degree is conferred and the date since the founding of Harvard College. Mom hugged me and gave me a motherly kiss; she was proud of her son. My life would never be the same.

A life-defining achievement, I looked forward to placing my Harvard diploma in the living room at our home in Mexican Canyon. This was a momentous event in my life; one that I had dreamt about. I still remember the countless hours of reading journal articles and writing research papers; I remember all the professors who helped me reach this significant milestone in my life. The academic year had gone by quickly. I was looking forward to meeting the parents of my colleagues at Cronkhite who were also graduating.

Shortly after returning to Arizona, I noticed that Dad was slowing down. He no longer wanted to walk up to the gate after dinner, something we always did. He said that he would have attended graduation, but he did not feel well. He reminded me that he hoped that he could have studied at Yale. But not graduating from high school was a major setback for him; his immediate obligation was to help the family financially. I noticed that Dad did not look well, but he was not one to complain.

When Dad became extremely ill, we took him to the Veteran's Hospital in Tucson. He was transferred to a nursing home where he seemed to be regaining his health. To me, he looked physically fit. When I visited him, he would ask me about Mackey Camp and Mexican Canyon. I looked forward to seeing him back home and walking up to the gate in the evenings. But he never made a full recovery, and he had a relapse. We rushed him to the Veterans Administration hospital. The last time I saw him was in the ICU where his life slowly ebbed away. Dad died on August 11, 1989.

I had hoped that Dad could have gone to visit me in Cambridge. While he preferred the rural life of Mackey Camp, he was always one to step out of his comfort zone. He would have remembered passing through New York on his way to England, France, and Germany. Certainly, he would have liked Cronkhite, where I lived. A harbor cruise would have been fun; maybe a short tour of the Yard would have been memorable with dinner at the faculty club. Maybe we would have encountered a national figure visiting Harvard.

I had the honor of meeting Ted Kennedy, who had graduated from Harvard College in 1956. I was in admiration of his many legislative accomplishments and his time as a presidential candidate. I had arrived an hour early at Longfellow Hall for his speech; I looked forward to listening to him talk about national policy matters. To my amazement he came out on stage early and was surprised to see me; he had a panic-stricken look on his face. I remembered how his two brothers had been assassinated in public forums. To ease his nervousness, I quipped that most people only flee after they have had a chance to know me. He gained his composure and was sharing with me the extraordinary challenges of being a senator. He offered me a staff position in Washington when I graduated from Harvard. As Hector Avalos would fondly tell me, you never know who you will meet in Cambridge.

Standing on Brattle Street I saw Harvard President Derek Bok having a conversation with his wife. I stopped to admire this national figure from afar. Nodding toward me, he proceeded to explain to his wife that students from around the world attend Harvard. I knew that I never would have the opportunity to greet him as a colleague. I wanted to share with him that I was a Chicano from Mexican Canyon, and I wanted to thank him for his exceptional leadership of a world-class university.

During my first year of residency, I supported a National Council of La Raza initiative to enact a Hispanic education executive order to address the undereducation of Latino students. On April 26, 1990, Harvard MEChA submitted a policy paper entitled *Assessing the Federal Response to the Undereducation of Hispanics* to the Department of Education. It was proposed that the Departments of Education and Labor establish a federal commission of Latino leaders and researchers to study the problem. It was recommended that Raul Yzaguirre, NCLR CEO, be selected to serve as chairperson of this federal commission. Executive Order 12729 was signed by President George Bush on September 24, 1990. I was the conceptual architect of the White House Commission on Hispanic Education. Shortly after its establishment, I received a note dated July 9, 1993, from the Executive Director providing me a progress report on the goals that embraced the America 2000 education strategy.

From time to time, I would get calls from people who were applying to Harvard or MIT. They wanted assistance formulating a plan that would help them prepare to write a dissertation. My advice included the following suggestions: Learn to write well and publish at least one article in an academic journal. Take one course in finite math, probability, and statistics. I noted that students can pursue either quantitative or qualitative research. Select one area of research as it is almost impossible to acquire expertise in both areas of research. Students who wish to conduct quantitative research should arrive at Harvard with a master's degree in statistics. Students who wish to pursue qualitative research should have four courses in English composition, four courses in sociology, four courses in history, four courses in policy studies, four courses in anthropology, four courses in government, two classes in organizational theory and behavior, and four courses in psychology. Read published Harvard dissertations as well as books published by Harvard professors. A student should obtain the reading list of the academic department before arriving at Harvard.

My memory of the Harvard coursework has faded with time. Doctoral students were required to maintain at least an A-minus average. I must admit I was overwhelmed by the amount of reading and required academic papers. I was always mindful that employers are intensely interested in college transcripts. College transcripts give a sense of the potential work contribution of applicants. When I look at my transcripts, they lack the detailed insight of the concerted effort needed to complete the classes. Nor do they give any indication of the numerous academic papers submitted for careful review by Harvard professors. I would be remiss if I did not give my impression of the classes listed on my Harvard transcript.

A013 Inquiry I. While apprehensive on the first day, I did very well in this class. Sitting at computer terminals, most of the class looked bewildered at their usage. The class was introduced to the SOS text editing program as preparation for writing statistical programs in SAS. I was highly proficient in using this text editor and joined the instructors teaching my classmates the various commands. In this course, we learned to use conditional probability for decision making. We were introduced to basic statistical concepts used in the social sciences.

A014 Inquiry II. I did well in this class. This course was a continuation of Inquiry I. We used Minitab statistical software to analyze large data sets. We learned how researchers used the High School and Beyond study to understand why schools were failing across the country. The professor should have spent three weeks examining the methodological issues that were raised about the Coleman report by analysis presented within *On Equality of Educational Opportunity: Papers Deriving From the Harvard University Faculty Seminar on the Coleman Report* (1972). Using inferential models, we learned to cast data in visual displays and looked at gender, educational level, socioeconomic status, and demographics. We learned to incorporate exogenous variables into our regression equations.

A021 Organization: Theory & Behavior. I did very well in this class. I found the study of complex organizations — multilevel organizations — extremely useful. We began the class by taking the Briggs Myers Personality Test. I was not surprised that the test profiled me as an essentially introverted person. The theory of complex organizations was examined in detail. Bolman and Deal's four frames of structure, human resource, political, and symbolic frames were central to the course. We learned about theory x and theory y, which explained employee motivation in the workplace. We used SWOT (strengths, weaknesses, opportunities, and threats) analysis to assess organizations. Each student wrote a case study to analyze an organization to which they had belonged. I picked the U.S. Army because it was an important life experience. We analyzed Harvard Business School case studies. I enjoyed this class so much that I wrote an additional paper.

A037 Financial Management & Control. I did well in this class. I considered this course to be a bread-and-butter course. Certainly, someday I would be managing million-dollar budgets. This course covered finance, accounting, and economics. This course was taught by a hedge fund manager who looked the part of the upper-class elite. This course could have been improved by adding two lectures on personal finance. The professor warned the class about the nefarious agenda of philistines. Later he became a college president.

A123 Politics of Higher Education. I passed this class. The professor did not make much effort to teach this class. Since I did not have an idea of what he wanted in an academic paper, I struggled more with academic writing than with the concepts. When I asked about why my performance was dismal, I was advised that I could not use anecdotal accounts to justify major points. We never read model journal articles that would guide our research efforts.

T620 Graduate Writing. This was a free non-credit course. A lot of students enrolled in this class. I guess I was not the only one worried about academic writing. A professor demonstrated the writing process from an initial idea. He elaborated on the importance of editing and revision. I had hoped that we would be invited to share our written work with him. Writing is a process that requires careful reflection.

A024 Education and Politics of the Policy Process. I did well in this class. This course was in the top three classes I took at Harvard. I applied to Harvard to learn the policy concepts presented in this course. We were fortunate that a national public policy scholar was teaching the class. He had conducted foundational work on bureaucracy and written many journal articles. The readings included topics on social policy, inequality, public governance, the role of pressure and protest groups, the nature of executive power, political language and symbols, social mobility, and the role of data analysis. Many of the articles were abstract. The professor was meticulously organized and bundled the policy articles together.

I found *Policy Paradox and Political Reason* (1988), a book by Deborah A. Stone, invaluable in understanding the conceptual framework of policy studies. I was impressed with the work of Elmer Eric Schattschneider, an influential policy academician. He wrote *Semi-Sovereign People* (1960), a highly regarded book on the political process. It explained why public institutions do not respond well to perplexing problems. My favorite quote from this book, "The flaw in a pluralist heaven is that the heavenly chorus sings with a strong upper-class accent." Remarkably like Percy Bysshe Shelley's observation, "The rich get richer and the poor get poorer."

One of the first journal articles that I read was *The Culture of Public Problems* (1981) by Joseph R. Gusfield, a noted sociologist from the University of Chicago. The introductory sentence read, "The use of the automobile is a microcosm on a large scale of the problems created by the conflict of restraint and release in American life." I wondered if my classmates were clear about the meaning of this sentence; I was not sure where the author was going with this assertion. After several readings, I translated this sentence to mean: While cars are problematic at times, they are central to our way of life. I wondered how writing instructors would improve the readability of Gusfield's introductory sentence?

S030 Intermediate Statistics. I did well in this class that had a school-wide reputation of being brutal on your grade point average. A key concept that stayed with me was that compensatory education works — contrary to what Arthur Jensen wrote in 1969. The Harvard statisticians disavowed the theory of eugenics, the controversial theory of genetics. They noted that Francis Galton was the father of statistical correlation.

The statisticians worked hard to take the sting out of learning the subject matter. The professors provided access to model academic papers in the library. But can you imagine a statistician who can entertain you with a funny comedy routine related to linear regression analysis? Many of the handouts had insightful cartoons about statistics.

We were introduced to Cyril Burt's twin data set taken from an Arthur Jensen journal article in *Behavioral Genetics* (1974). The twins were separated into two groups. One group of growing up in their natural home and a second group of growing in a foster home. The utility of descriptive statistics and scatterplots was demonstrated. Then we were instructed in how the Least Squares Regression Line is constructed and its correlation relationship. At the time I did not know that Cyril Burt had been accused of falsifying his data.

Harvard professors constructed regression equations to predict academic achievement. We learned that socioeconomic background could account for 50 percent of academic achievement. When you add one parent's income, about 70 percent of academic achievement can be accounted for. The professors warned us of the danger of adding collinear variables, such as combining a father's income and mother's income. The professors noted that this statistical incongruity might have skewed the *Coleman report* (1966) conclusion that school funding does not make a difference. Curiously, they did not mention the controversy surrounding the measurement of human intelligence. The class was blessed to have exceptional statistics instructors.

When presented with a problem in policy studies, the initial step is to understand its societal impact. In a quantitative study, selecting a random sample from the population, or a list of pertinent data, is paramount. We used the SAS statistical package to do all the heavy lifting. The DO STATISTICS command produced a large number of descriptive statistics. The SAS software was extremely good at performing analysis of variance and linear regression. Using the general linear model, we learned to construct multiple regression models. PROC REG command was used for statistical modeling to make causal inferences between the independent and dependent variables.

I experienced my first academic crisis when I was awarded an F on the first S030 test. I went into a panic; I was determined not to flunk out of this course. Recording the class lecturers provided the means to remember important statistical concepts needed in our papers. This was a challenging course for me, but I passed it with a good grade.

A205 Microeconomics: *Lens for Understanding Education Policy Issues*. I did well in this class. This was another bread-and-butter course. A central concept of the course was that college graduates earn twice as much as non-college graduates. Understanding monetary policy is a prerequisite to developing public policy. We were given ten problem sets to solve. Our recommendations to fictional government officials were contained in memorandums. Topics included financing higher education, shortage of math and science teachers, the value of college education, cost of running a consulting firm, cost for elementary and secondary education, and cost-benefit analysis. Many of my memos were scored excellent. I hoped to learn how to develop a durable competitive advantage within my investments.

S052 Applied Data Analysis. I did very well in this class. Building on concepts learned in S-030, we explored a wide range of statistical techniques. We were introduced to the methods needed to analyze social data. We learned about the pitfalls of stepwise regression. We were introduced to logistic regression and submitted five statistical papers. Students embraced Rupert Miller's dictum of the utility of reporting a p-value as a measure of the credibility of the null hypothesis. As part of the S052 class, we took a pledge to use the word estimated when referring to a sample statistic, include discussion of the population in any reference to a null hypothesis, and on no occasion inappropriately banter around the concept of statistical significance —certainly never in an elevator located on the Harvard campus.

A222 Higher Education and the Law. I passed this course. An essential course to surviving in colleges and universities, we examined the structure of our jurisprudence system; we engaged in thinking about the law in pragmatic ways. We were introduced to the concepts of estoppel, the fruit of the poisonous tree, and the doctrine of dirty hands. We discussed the importance of academic freedom for professors and students. We read about a thousand cases that gave us a solid understanding of the law. I read the Federalist Papers as an independent study. Interestingly, the professor made provocative observations about stellar Harvard Law professors.

S510 Introduction to Field Research Methods. I did well in this fascinating research course. We were introduced to ethnography to understand culture and society. Using the participant observation approach, I enjoyed the initial assignment of watching the hustle and bustle of Harvard Square. Anthropologists have used qualitative methods to study ancient civilizations and cultural groups. Qualitative research attempts to understand the context of the human condition. The researcher conducts a study by observing, listening, and conversing with informants to understand their situation. We learned the necessity of obtaining informed consent before talking to a research subject. As fledging researchers, we acquired methods on how to understand informants' lives. We learned the importance of validity and reliability measures. The professor requested that students refrain from asking questions during the course, so I never asked him a question about qualitative research. I always wondered why he ever aspired to be a teacher.

T440 Teaching and Learning. I received a wonderful grade in this class. A central aspect of the course was to observe the moon to discover the cyclic nature of lunar orbits. The course encouraged students to explore unfamiliar ideas. Many years later I used the T440 concepts to teach Chinese numerals to college students. Chinese characters were always a mystery to me; I had no context to understand them or their usage. I had to gain a basic level of understanding when I decided to teach college students how to depict Chinese numerals; I presented the opportunity to learn Chinese numerals as a wonderful idea. We explored how to write Chinese numerals and how to perform basic numerical calculations; this section was both challenging and fun for me and the students. I had my students write the Chinese numeral zero on a whiteboard. You could almost see their minds working away as they visualized the numeral; they enjoyed the physicality of sketching out the symbol. I came to appreciate the T440 course for many reasons.

A090 Approaching Research. I did not receive credit for this class. What a disappointment. I still do not understand the disconnect between myself and the professor. This course was an introduction to writing the thesis proposal, which must be approved by the Committee on Degrees before you can start writing the dissertation. We were even provided an outline for the proposal. What could go wrong? I had a strong visceral reaction the day I received my A090 grade. The grade was recorded as INP with no credit earned; for all practical purposes, this grade was an F. What is maddening is I never received any feedback about my work. In hindsight, I did not have a clear research question with the appropriate research methodology. Perhaps the professor could have explained how to select a research question and discuss the appropriate research mythology. This setback would be corrected when I moved on to the dissertation stage.

A095 Integrative Seminar. I did well in this course. This was a capstone course for doctoral students. This course was to examine the role of education in society. Prominent leaders were invited to share their experiences with the class. Michael Dukakis, a former Democratic presidential candidate, presented his views on educational policy and national politics. Howard Gardner, The John H. and Elisabeth A. Hobbs Research Professor of Cognition and Education, provided a comprehensive explanation of his theory of Multiple Intelligences. Two analytical papers were required for this course. I learned that I needed to expand my decision-making capacity. I appreciated that the professor, known to be a hard-nosed lawyer, was patient with me.

H440 Design for Learning: An Integrative Seminar. I did well in this course and was inspired by the professor on the art of teaching. This course was in the top three classes I took at Harvard. He posited that knowledge is generative; I admired his insights into teaching. In terms of student learning, he proposed that students embrace the retention of knowledge. I came to understand the reasons why the learning process was problematic for me. Now when I hear about failing students, I turn to his thoughtful insights on learning.

S060 Analyzing Categorical (and Ordinal) Data. I did extremely well in this class. My research colleague was an international student from China. The statistical techniques I learned in this class were applied to study the effects of inequality. In studying social mobility, the important categories are high school diplomas, bachelor's degrees, master's degrees, and doctoral degrees. SAS software was useful in building regression models for categorical data. Constructing contingency tables, we used the logit function to analyze categorical data. We also used the Shapiro-Wilk test to detect atypical data points. When examining non-linear plots, we used Tukey's ladder. Residual analysis was key to dealing with heteroscedasticity.

A999 Special Readings or Research in Admin, Plan, Social Policy. I enjoyed reading the research textbooks that helped me write my dissertation and prepare me for a policy position at a university or government office. On the policy side, John W. Kingdon's *Agendas, Alternatives, and Public Policies* (1984) is a must reading to understand why the government is slow to respond to constituent needs. *Making Public Policy* by Steven Kelman (1987) is a step-by-step approach to policymaking. This book examines the limits of the presidency. *A Primer for Policy Analysis* (1978) by Edith Stokey and Richard Zeckhauser provides insight into using linear programming for policy analysis. *Data Analysis for Politics and Policy* by Edward R. Tufte (1974) was useful in selecting statistical techniques. *Qualitative Data Analysis* (1983) by Matthew B. Miles and A. Michael Huberman was a great sourcebook for qualitative research. *Reliability and Validity in Qualitative Research* (1985) by Jerome Kirk and Marc L. Miller looks at two important concepts in research. *Case Study Research* by Robert K. Yin (1984) discusses the case study as a research strategy.

X002 Analytic Paper. I was fortunate to have a dream team of national scholars guiding my work on the dissertation. My advisor is a caring person who assembled a dedicated dissertation committee. These professors are stellar researchers; I appreciated that they attenuated the meddling tendencies by other professors. They assisted me to address the requested revisions mandated by the Committee on Degrees (COD).

Many of the doctoral students disliked the oversight of the Committee on Degrees, which was composed of leading scholars who conduct research. In their July 13, 1994, letter the COD warned me of serious consequences for not completing my coursework within six years; the Harvard faculty could drop me as a student. Working full-time did not make matters easier. Many faculty and students looked to me to participate in college committees.

On May 6, 1996, the Committee on Degrees notified me that the analytic paper proposal was accepted. However, interrater reliability was one issue that I needed to address. The COD was forever putting pressure on me to finish my thesis — something I appreciated immensely.

I was pleased that I would sit for my doctoral defense on Friday, June 28, 1996. I found my way to Gutman Library but was understandably nervous answering questions about my research effort. It was an interesting experience to have a room full of Harvard professors asking questions about the nature of research. I met with my advisor and committee members and answered questions about conducting biographical research. To avoid systematic biases, I agreed to have two independent researchers review the transcripts. I reflected on my own biases through personal notes as part of the research process.

On December 17, 1996, I submitted a Memorandum of Understanding, which outlined how I would conduct research. My research took me across the country to cities with large Latino populations. Los Angeles, Phoenix, San Antonio, Chicago, Washington D.C., and Miami, Florida hosted Latino leadership conferences. I observed national Latino leaders discuss important policy issues. I kept a contact summary form that highlighted the substantive steps in data collection.

I received a letter dated July 10, 1997, that I had exceeded the seven-year limit for completing a doctoral degree. I was grateful that the COD gave me an extension. Yet, I reached a point where I did not think I was going to finish a doctorate at Harvard and would have to settle for a less demanding doctoral program. I was blessed; there were countless times when my advisor and dissertation committee encouraged me to finish.

On March 13, 1998, the Committee on Degrees notified me that I had passed my oral examination; my memorandum of understanding was on file. This was the final hurdle that I needed to complete. I was fortunate that I did not have any dissertation revisions to complete. The COD closed with, "Best of luck as you proceed with your dissertation and work toward your graduation!"

On September 23, 1998, I received a kind letter from one of my committee members who I admire for her high academic standards. She wrote, "The biographical portraits are better balanced with each other, in sharper focus, and more clearly and smoothly composed allowing the reader to see both the individuality and unique qualities of each as well as the cross-cutting themes that you underscore in the final chapter."

On October 1, 1998, I received a letter from a committee member who raised a pointed question about one of my biographical portraits. One intriguing question which was posed to me was, Can a Latino leader be socially liberal but economically conservative? It was not obvious to me at the time, but a Chicano or Latina leader needs money to fuel the organization. Successful leaders need money to establish infrastructure and effective programs to ultimately achieve their goals.

Harvard University officially conferred the doctorate on November 17, 1998. I was elated with the news; I had accomplished the impossible. I extended my deepest appreciation to my dissertation subjects who were generous with their time. I was extremely thankful that my dissertation committee helped me overcome the academic barriers, and mindful of all the people who helped me reach this milestone.

I contemplated having a single embossed page with the gold leaf Latin word *Veritas* on the introductory page of my dissertation. Recognized as the official seal, *Veritas* encompasses a timeless academic legacy that is unique to Harvard. The original dictum was *Veritas In Christi Gloriam,* according to Harvard records. A Harvard historical document noted that the crimson shield was depicted in a Harvard Corporation document dated December 27, 1643. Harvard records indicate that for a brief period *Veritas* was replaced with *Christo et Ecclesiae*. *Veritas* evokes an enduring fidelity to the academic values of scholars.

The title of my dissertation is *Hispanic Leadership: The Lives of Four Mexican-American Leaders*. I hoped that Chicana and Chicano studies programs would approve of my dissertation. The OCLC WorldCat® lists my dissertation being housed at several colleges and universities: Harvard College Library, Harvard University, Harvard University Archives, University of California Davis, University Santa Barbara, San Diego State University Library, University of New Mexico – Main Campus, and *El Colegio de México*. The Spanish descriptor is *Líderes mexicanoamericanos – Biografías*.

While my dissertation was an ethnographic study of Mexican-American leadership, its subtext was the paradox of opportunity. I noted that Latinos are skeptical of the notion of equal employment opportunity. The promise of equal opportunity goes to those with a remarkable employment track record, strong interpersonal skills, and exceptional academic credentials. Yet, the small number of *raza* in executive positions is an indication that the paradox of opportunity is a limiting condition affecting *raza* applicants. Consequently, Latinos who work in multilevel organizations have a pragmatic understanding of organizational parameters that define their position.

February 11, 1998, was one of my happiest days. I sent Mom a graduation announcement that I would be graduating with a Harvard doctorate. My brief note said, "Dear Mom, I am writing to let you know I am thinking of you every day. Thank you for all your encouragement and support while I was studying at Harvard. Love, Your son, Ernesto."

Student debt would be my concern for the next twenty years. I was extremely fortunate that I was teaching full-time and was paying into a pension plan. I did not worry about my economic situation anymore. I borrowed $44,430 from Harvard University and paid it off in December 2006. While my Harvard education cost about $75,000 — best ballpark estimation, I saw this expenditure as a good investment. I was relieved when I made my last payment on my student loans in 2013.

Graduating Harvard students elect their class marshal to carry the academic banner. On graduation day, I was walking toward the assembly area for graduates when I was stopped by a Harvard official who handed me the 1999 class banner. She said that I was selected to lead my graduating class. I was surprised and honored with my new role during commencement. My favorite graduation photo is the one of me carrying the class banner on graduation day.

After the graduation ceremony, Mom and I walked over to the statue of John Harvard located in the Yard. We joined Harvardians from around the world to pay homage to this visionary minister. The statue seemed to be a stylized rendition of a 17th century New England male. Looking at the bronze statue, I remember thinking, "Thank you John Harvard for letting me study at your world-class university." All my dreams and professional goals seemed to coalesce at this moment in time. My life was forever changed and the journey from Mexican Canyon was complete.

The coursework was demanding, and the dissertation required time to assemble a research agenda. Studying at Harvard was both exhausting and exhilarating. Finally, I felt that my life was on track and I would have many professional opportunities. I was hoping that someday I would have the opportunity to teach Chicano and Chicana studies. I had little interest in discussing my doctorate from Harvard. Talking about earning a Harvard degree is a two-edged sword. Some people resent when an individual can obtain the brass ring of academic achievement; others acknowledge the distinctiveness of academic accomplishment. I felt ready to teach or work at any college or university. But all of that was behind me; I looked forward to continuing my role as a college teacher.

"From my experiences, I have learned that if you have a dream, God has given you the ability to make that dream come true. If someone tells you differently, they are absolutely wrong."

— Cleopatria Martínez, Ph.D., College Mathematics Professor

6

COLLEGE TEACHER

EVERY PROFESSOR REMEMBERS THEIR FIRST TEACHING POSITION. Teaching at the college level was a life aspiration, and I brought a wealth of life experiences and academic preparation to the table. I enjoyed the aspectual, theoretical contours of mathematics and working with students who were preparing for the future. More importantly, I would be helping students who had tentative feelings about mathematics. It was gratifying working with older students who were genuinely interested in learning. They valued the notion that education would personally improve them and open doors of opportunity in the workplace.

Sitting in my office, that first day of classes, I remembered the peacefulness of Mexican Canyon. Mom was pleased that I had landed a good job, and shared the good news with friends and relatives. Just the year before, Dad had passed away. I wondered what he would say about my career working at a college. Certainly, he would have been pleased that I was teaching mathematics. I intended to make a positive difference in the lives of my students.

Every semester I looked forward to meeting my students and shared with them that I had many life experiences including washing dishes, working in the copper mines, manning a missile system in the military, and extensive experience teaching math. Somehow, I had to let the students know that I understood their apprehension of mathematics. I explained that successful students must have *ganas* to learn mathematics. I advised them that with focused desire they would be able to pass any college class. Some of the students were astonished that I had graduated from Harvard; I only acknowledged that it was a life-changing experience.

On January 17, 1991, President George H. W. Bush announced to the world the start of Desert Storm, the military push to remove Saddam Hussein from Kuwait. CNN showed footage of the Baghdad night sky lighting up with anti-aircraft fire. I knew that Patriot missile batteries of the 32nd Army Air and Missile Defense Command were protecting Israel against Scud missile attacks being fired by Iraq. The soldiers who manned the missile systems were trained at Fort Bliss. From the comfort of an office, I prayed for their families and their safety. Now my vocation was teaching undergraduate mathematics and serving on college committees.

Right away I was given important math departmental duties. Accreditation is crucial to both the department and college; during my first year, I was assigned to write a math department assessment narrative that would satisfy NCA accreditation requirements. I encouraged the chairperson that each math course is assessed by a common final for all courses taught at the college. A math course average could be computed for each math course for that semester. Each semester the math course average could provide evidence on how much students were learning. More importantly, any salient instructional weakness could be identified and given immediate attention from the math faculty.

I was mindful that all college students wanted to move forward in their lives. I had a special bond with the Chicano students; many of them were just like me. They came from a *barrio* remarkably like Mexican Canyon. I would always tell them, "Chart your destiny and never give up. *¡Sí se puede!*" They would share their hopes for the future and life challenges; they were determined to succeed.

Teaching does not occur in a vacuum. After a busy day of teaching, I was appalled by the videotaped beating by Los Angeles Police Department officers of Rodney King, which was aired on March 3, 1991. I was asked by Mechistas how this could happen in a civil society. All I could tell them is that our country has a judicial system based on due process; those with authority had the obligation to protect all citizens. Expressing what many people felt, President George H. W. Bush was disgusted by the actions of the L.A. police officers. When the police officers were acquitted of all charges on April 29, 1992, black Angelenos were outraged with the verdict. Predictably, rioting erupted in L.A. that night with dozens of businesses set on fire.

César Chávez was awarded an honorary doctorate at Arizona State University in 1992; he looked so majestic in his doctoral regalia. I have so many memories of his leadership role in the United Farmworkers Union, and I attended many of his social justice demonstrations. He energized farmworkers to follow him and boycott work in the vineyards. With union power, he was able to negotiate labor contracts with growers. Like many Chicanos, he completed only the

8th grade in school. President Bill Clinton awarded César Chávez the Medal of Freedom posthumously in 1994.

I gave Mechistas my view of the development of Chicano issues. I explained that the Chicano Movement was a logical extension of the Mexican-American era. *La Chicanada* did not see themselves just working as laborers. Chicanos were vitally interested in obtaining an education that would lead to professional positions. *Raza* was interested in city government jobs, some saw opportunity in the military, others with an entrepreneurial spirit selected business careers, and in my case I hoped for and achieved an academic career. But American institutions seemed closed to admitting *raza*. Public law prohibited discrimination, but we saw its effects. Our struggle revolved around the central aim of gaining social and economic equality. I challenged MEChA to be engaged in issues like supporting Chicana and Chicano studies, civil rights, Dreamers, immigration, voter registration, bilingual education, and affirmative action. When it counts, I noted that college students have the energy and power to effectuate social change.

When the opportunity presented itself, I would talk to Mechistas about the legacy of prominent Chicano/Chicana leaders. I had great admiration for the following Chicano leadership: César Chávez lived and worked in both Arizona and California as a labor leader; Dolores Huerta was instrumental in the farmworker struggle; Raul Yzaguirre was CEO of the National Council of la Raza (NCLR) who addressed the undereducation of Latinos; Willie Velásquez is remembered for initiating the Southwest Voter Registration Education Project in 1974; Rodolfo "Corky" Gonzales was a leader in the Crusade for Justice in Denver Colorado; Leyla Catán was a television journalist in Tucson who investigated employment discrimination; José Ángel Gutiérrez established La Raza Unida Party as a third political party; Dr. Cleopatria Martínez was Arizona Association of Chicanos in Higher Education president; Dr. Hector P. Garcia founded the American G.I. Forum to fight discrimination; Dr. Christine Marín is an archivist, historian, and community activist in Phoenix; Reies Lopez Tijerina fought for Spanish land grants in New Mexico; Janet Murguia is CEO of Unidos US, a Latino civil rights organization in Washington DC; Isabel Garcia is an immigration lawyer in Tucson; Dr. Manuel de Jesús Hernandez-G, a national scholar in Chicano studies, was effective in addressing social justice as a policy issue; and, Danny Ortega is an activist lawyer in Phoenix.

My deepest respect was reserved for Mechistas who had served in the military. They stepped up to serve their country when others elected to attend college. I encouraged them to take leadership roles in MEChA. I shared with them the ignoble historical event that Texas refused to allow the burial of Felix Z. Longoria, a World War II casualty, who died on the island of Luzon, the Philippines in June 1945. The controversy of his internment in Three Rivers, Texas occurred in 1949 when the local funeral home would not conduct a funeral service for Pvt. Longoria. The funeral home director said that *raza* did not know how to attend services respectfully. Senator Lyndon Baines Johnson facilitated Longoria's interment at Arlington National Cemetery.

The reification of mathematical concepts was my goal. I used red, green, blue, and black markers to sketch out math problems. I related that I always enjoyed learning mathematics. Or I would tell them how Bart Simpson hated math word problems. When I sketched out the unit circle, I complained that it looked more like a lopsided tortilla. I always thought it was a mistake not to interject some humor before diving into the abstract landscape of mathematics. But the students who liked my classes were students who were themselves parents. They shared with me that they used my approach and logic in helping their children learn math. Essentially, they focused on having fun with math as the key to motivate their children in school. Their kids now saw their parents in a different light; the parents delighted in being elevated to superstar status.

Many of the students had a complimentary sobriquet for me; they would call me Mr. Escalante, after the famed Bolivian educator who was depicted in the movie *Stand and Deliver* (1988). He taught at Garfield High School, which was one of the low-performing high schools in Los Angeles. I was humbled that my students saw me in the same light. I thought that the word problem, illustrated in the movie, was instructive. In the movie, the students read the problem out loud, "Juan has five times as many girlfriends as Pedro. Carlos has one girlfriend less than Pedro. The total number of girlfriends between them is twenty. How many girlfriends does each gigolo have?" When the students asked me to solve the problem, I would tell them to go see the movie. They would enjoy the problem-solving skills of the students as they grappled with the problem. Jaime Escalante excelled in teaching AP calculus to supposedly math underachievers. I enjoyed the *Stand and Deliver* scene where Escalante teaches his students to use tabular integration.

Perhaps the most difficult aspect of teaching is issuing a failing grade. I had to fail *raza*. Some of them did not come to class or study for exams. On one occasion I had a young man stop trying or was overwhelmed by the coursework. He did not withdraw from the math class after I advised him of his abysmal academic performance. His friends in the class tried to get him to withdraw. As I had predicted, he ended up with an F for the term grade. A few weeks later my student had the seat next to me on the same flight to El Paso, Texas, during the semester break. What were the chances of this happening? I said, "Hi." And he, in turn, greeted me. It was a tense hour-long trip for me and the student. The student had stopped coming to class and never sought help from me.

On the flip side, I have had students acknowledge my teaching. I remember one student say, "I can't tell you enough how much I appreciate you taking the time to help me. Before my class ended last semester, I was asking for advice on what teacher I could sign up for when several students and teachers told me of a certain teacher. They told me there is this really wonderful teacher and they recommended you. I know God was watching over me when I ran into you in the hall. I'm excited about being in your class and learning something that has always been a challenge for me. I really want to be good at math more than anything. I don't know you, but I know for a fact that you have touched many people's lives." This testimonial is emblematic of the memories that I will never forget.

I enjoyed teaching the survey of mathematics course, the terminal course for liberal arts students. The question was, "What should an undergraduate know upon completing this type of course?" The question is almost impossible to answer. Certainly, mathematical reasoning is useful in everyday life. When I taught this course, it covered set theory, systems of numeration, the mathematics of investments, statistics, probability, graph theory, and topology.

I liked teaching the section on personal finance, which covered investments, loans, mortgages, and stocks. I advised students to pay themselves first and live below their means. I encouraged students to read *Rich Dad Poor Dad: What the Rich Teach Their Kids about Money*

—That the Poor and Middle Class Do Not! (1977) by Robert T. Kiyosaki with Sharon L. Lechter. They observe, "The poor and the middle-class work for money. The rich have money work for them." I wanted students to watch Suzy Orem on PBS or Jim Cramer's Mad Money television program. I also required them to read anything that Warren Buffet had written about financial investment as well as David and Tom Gardner's Motley Fool column. Dave Ramsey provides timely advice to those who are struggling with financial planning. I pointed out that a fifteen-year house mortgage was the ideal next to paying cash for a house. I warned them that Social Security would probably not be around when they reached retirement age. We spent time making present value and future value calculations using the TI-83 calculator. Their final exam consisted of developing a financial plan that would lead to a million-dollar retirement fund.

When Google filed a $2.7 billion initial public offering on April 30, 2004, with the Federal Trade Commission, I mentioned to my students that the filing paid tribute to the number e. It was reported that the exact offering was $2,718,281,828. Some students asked me whether to buy Google stock; the stock was selling for about $130 a share. I told them that anyone with a background in investing was buying the stock. Now I wished I had advised my students to buy the stock if they had the money.

In the world of financial investments, I implored students to pay careful attention to the astounding power of the compounding effect. Legend has it that Albert Einstein was asked what mankind's greatest invention was. He purportedly answered by saying it was compound interest. With the expectation that financial turbulence will eventually occur in our lives, I would tell my students to save as little as five percent of the money earned each month. I cautioned students to safeguard their money; the Shakespearian character Polonius in *Hamlet* warned, "Neither a borrower nor a lender be."

Most students have a fascination with infinity; I noted that infinity is certainly one of the more intriguing concepts in mathematics. Lewis Carroll, author of *Alice's Adventures in Wonderland*, perhaps in a whimsical moment, perceived that a second is longer than infinity. Mathematicians have not stopped debating the nature of infinity. I emphasized to my students that infinity is not a number, but more an idea of boundless quantity, a notion that is advanced by Math World. When teaching a survey of mathematics class, I devoted a week of lectures on the work of Georg Cantor related to his development of infinite sets and transfinite numbers. I stressed that cardinality is important to grasp the concept of aleph-null, an infinite number, symbolized $\aleph_0$. For transfinite numbers, the equation $\aleph_0 + \aleph_0 = \aleph_0$, is paradoxically true. The students were spellbound with the notion of levels of infinity.

I was asked by the math department chairperson to help colleagues who were struggling with teaching. I found that scaffolding math concepts were essential to the teaching process. I emphasized that math instructors must establish a personal connection with students — it is not enough to just be a talking head. I explained that I used metaphors to teach math concepts. Students should have the opportunity to engage the instructor in a conversation about mathematics to clear up misconceptions. Encouragement goes a long way. When it comes to teaching, caring about student success defines the exceptional teacher. In my classes I encouraged students to become active learners. I found that explaining math in everyday terms was helpful.

While I was writing my dissertation, Christopher Jencks penned his highly polemical book *Rethinking Social Policy: Race, Poverty, and the Underclass* (1992). He is Malcolm Wiener Professor of Social Policy at the Kennedy School of Government, Harvard University. Starting with Social Security, Jencks provides a comprehensive view of social policy. He examined affirmative action, the social safety net, inequality, crime, urban ghettos, welfare, and the expanding underclass. He observed, "Johnson's Great Society programs were mainly concerned with helping the poor rise in the world." With the publication of the Coleman report, his views changed. Jencks believed that "…we could not eliminate poverty simply by doubling or tripling everyone's income." The establishment of a safety net, according to Jencks, was opposed by conservatives. I wondered who could be opposed to social services that keep families out of the poor house? Jencks conceded the failure of President Reagan's trickle-down economics, where the poor are helped when the rich reap financial rewards. Citing *Ethnic America* (1981), Jencks wrongly declared that Mexican Americans immigrated to the United States. As Chicano historians observe, "We did not cross the U.S. border, the U.S. border crossed us." While acknowledging his status as a Harvard professor, I do not think that I could ever endorse his ideas.

Late on Friday, April 23, 1993, I learned that César Chávez had passed away. I remembered the massive demonstrations where *raza* assembled to hear him talk about dire working conditions in the agricultural fields and the importance of supporting the grape boycott. His insistence on non-violent protest inspired his followers. On that day, I thought he was too young to die. I still remember his view on education, "Real education should consist of drawing the goodness and the best out of our own students. What better books can there be than the book of humanity?" I spoke to Mechistas who knew of his struggle for farmworker's rights. In the Southwest many schools, buildings, and streets are named after this great leader. The U.S. Navy commissioned the USNS Cesar Chavez on May 5, 2012. President Bill Clinton conferred the Medal of Freedom on César Chávez on August 8, 1994. I believe that now is the time to establish a national holiday to honor this national leader.

On June 24, 1993, mathematicians were astonished by the announcement that Fermat's Last Theorem had been proven. This theorem had mystified mathematicians for three centuries. Professor Andrew Wiles of Princeton University was able to prove that there were no solutions for the equation + for n greater than 2. The legendary quest began with Fermat complaining that there was not enough room in the margin of his book to write the proof. The fascination with mathematics in popular culture highlights its centrality in society. In the immensely popular television series Star Trek, five centuries in the future Captain Jean-Luc Picard attempts to prove Fermat's Last Theorem.

Around this time, the action thriller *Clear and Present Danger* (1994) was released. The antagonist is the drug lord Ernesto Escobedo. With a knowing smile, students and professors would mention this coincidence to me. The plot of the movie involved the Cali Cartel and ensuing U.S. intervention into Colombia. Jack Ryan is an intelligence officer who navigates the labyrinth of the federal government to fight governmental corruption. Jack Ryan cuts a deal with Ernesto Escobedo to save Army operators from captivity. But Ernesto Escobedo must die, which I have accepted with fatalistic equanimity. The movie deserved five stars.

My uncle came to visit me from Corpus Christi, Texas to give me a new book resplendent in crimson, red, purple, yellow, and blue hues — *The Bell Curve: Intelligence and Class Structure in American*

Life (1994), 845 pages. You could tell that he was troubled with the basic tenet of the book that *mexicanos* are dumb. I assured him that intelligence has many dimensions, which cannot be expressed solely as a single number. I smiled and said, *"Tío,* you and Dad didn't survive World War II because you were mentally deficient. Being successful in life doesn't boil down to an intelligence quotient." *The Bell Curve* resurrected the debate about the distribution of intelligence among racial groups. Richard J. Herrnstein, the lead author of this highly controversial study, was the Edgar Pierce Professor of Psychology at Harvard University. He received his Ph.D. from Harvard in 1955. In the manner of Frances Galton, Herrnstein appeared to erroneously believe that *raza* and other ethnic groups were deficient in intellectual capacity. I explained to my uncle that Harvard professors also theorize that socioeconomic background and parental occupation explain 70 percent of academic achievement.

When I was writing my dissertation, I turned to the historical work of Dr. Mario T. García, *Memories of Chicano History: The Life and Narrative of Bert Corona* (1994); this was an excellent source on the Chicano labor movement. The author and Bert Corona were both born in El Paso, Texas, a city that borders Mexico. With an encyclopedic knowledge of Mexican and American history, he wrote extensively on the Mexican-American generation. I wished I had had the opportunity to study under his tutelage; I spent an entire year reading Mexican history to write the third chapter of my dissertation, The Historical Context of the Study.

I enrolled in a qualitative research course taught by Dr. Raymond V. Padilla. After finishing two years of coursework at Harvard, I wondered how a Chicano professor would approach this academic subject. He was an exceptional professor and I nominated him for a teaching position at Harvard. He and Dr. Rudolfo Chávez Chávez had published a new book, *The Leaning Ivory Tower: Latino Professors in American Universities* (1995). The title could have easily been *The Paradox of Opportunity in Academia.* The authors noted, "Even though Latino and Latina academics may have been disoriented by covert and overt prejudices, marginalized, and made to question their humanity in the everyday experience of academic life, these individuals have instinctively reoriented themselves." Certainly, I could have submitted a chapter of a hostile work environment that I experienced. I wish that I would have cited their work in my dissertation. But somehow, I failed to use this work in my review of the literature. Despite an uneven playing field within academe, the authors give hope to new faculty members. The narratives are food for thought for university and college presidents.

Discussion of human intelligence was a lively topic with the publication of *Emotional Intelligence: Why it Can Matter More Than IQ* (1995) written by New York Times reporter Daniel Goleman. College professors and students were talking about a new definition of intelligence. Those human attributes of empathy, compassion, understanding, and kindness are the cornerstones of being a high performing person. These were human attributes that my *abuelitas* prized. Some of the social policy theorists were not convinced about the validity and theoretical foundation of emotional intelligence. I felt that it was important to acknowledge the importance of emotional intelligence in encouraging college students to succeed.

I greeted former presidential candidate Barry Goldwater, the standard-bearer of conservatism, on April 3, 1996, as a distinguished speaker at the college. Goldwater could no longer walk and used a wheelchair. His political base from Sun City came out to cheer him on. I remember him as the Republican presidential candidate in 1964 who served as the United States Senator from Arizona from January 3, 1969, to January 3, 1987. Arriving in a black limousine around 10 a.m., I also remembered him for voting against the Civil Rights Bill of 1964. But this day he looked forward to talking to college students. He gave insight into his political career and his service in World War II. Goldwater got one question about affirmative action, which he did not answer. He said that he had always aspired to be affirmative in life. Harvard awards the Barry Goldwater Scholarship to promising scholars, which is funded by the U.S. Government. Two years later he died on May 29, 1998.

Like many people, I did not pay attention to the launching of the Fox News station on October 7, 1996. Almost immediately it had a decidedly conservative view on national issues. It promoted its reporting as being fair and balanced. But when Fox News started criticizing MEChA and *raza*, I came to see this media outlet as the voice of the radical right. This television network seemed to promote dissonance within American society. But there is always that one journalist who understands national issues.

Originally with National Public Radio (NPR), Juan Williams brought a sense of hope and humanity to the Fox News channel. His reason and optimism resonated with many viewers. He is a prolific writer who writes about American history. A mainstay commentator on *The Five*, he battled the far-right agenda. On May 26, 2021, he announced his departure from *The Five*. I suspect that his thoughtful opinion was too much for Fox News. I hope to meet Juan Williams someday and discuss with him the struggle for social justice.

Another Fox News commentator, whom I admire, is Chris Wallace. A Harvard College graduate, he is a tenacious journalist who asks all the tough questions. He is the gadfly that asks the difficult question that other journalists do not ask. Wallace moderated the first presidential debate on Tuesday, September 29, 2020, at the Case Western Reserve University in Cleveland. By all accounts, the debate was contentious, and Wallace had a difficult time keeping the candidates on task. While political-focused conversations are stimulating, I would rather talk to Wallace about his Latino classmates at Harvard and educational opportunities.

Arturo Rosales published *Chicano! The History of the Mexican American Civil Rights Movement* in 1996, which traced the historical forces that changed the American social, cultural, and political landscape. Raul Yzaguirre, NCLR CEO, wore the red Chicano! publicity button during one of NCLR's annual conferences. The Chicano movement cascaded from California to Arizona that mobilized *raza* to protest discrimination. Arturo Rosales wonders about the legacy of the Chicano Movement. Theorists posit that the Chicano Movement is still the blueprint for social, economic, and political empowerment. I was pleasantly surprised that my good friend Salomón Baldenegro is pictured on page 211 of the history book. Sal is a Chicano intellectual who has rallied against unfair labor practices and was politically aligned with La Raza Unida Party.

I was at the end of completing my dissertation when Harvard professor Sara Lawrence-Lightfoot and Jessica Hoffmann Davis published *The Art and Science of Portraiture* in 1997. Beautifully written, this is an exemplary methodological book on qualitative research. The purpose of the book, in the words of Harvard professor Lawrence-Lightfoot, is "...to combine systematic, empirical description with aesthetic expression, blending art and science, humanistic sensibilities and scientific rigor." They pay homage to cultural anthropologist

Clifford Geertz, who developed the concept of "thick description" to capture the essence of the human experience. This masterpiece gives a clear representation of the research process.

On June 2, 1998, California residents passed Proposition 227 to repeal bilingual education. This is a deeply personal issue for many Mexican Americans. For sure, Chicanos view this legislative measure as oppressive. My *abuelitas* would have said that speaking both English and Spanish served the national interest. My Tío Lalo, an Army colonel, when speaking with his South American counterparts, represented the United States admirably when discussing military matters in Spanish. Raul Yzaguirre, former NCLR President, once observed, "By playing on mainstream fears about immigrants and distorting the facts about Hispanic Americans, they have awakened, encouraged, and provided for a surface legitimacy to racist and nativist sentiment."

The Mechistas were ready to travel to *El Día De La Raza* that was held on October 12, 1996, to protest Washington public policy. You could call (800) 410-12-96 to obtain an up-to-date agenda. The organizers focused on seven policy issues:

> "Human and Constitutional Rights for All.
>
> Equal Opportunities and Affirmative Action.
>
> Free Public Education for All, from, K-12 to the Universities.
>
> Expansion of Health Services.
>
> Citizen Police Review Boards.
>
> Labor Law Reform and $7.00 per Hour Minimal Wage.
>
> Citizenship Now and Extend the Date of Eligibility for Amnesty."

I thought that this trip was an important part of MEChA's college education. MEChA and Latinos from across the nation would be attending a national forum in Washington D.C. With limited financial resources, MEChA would engage in full-court fundraising. I encouraged them to talk to their teachers about their trip expenses. The day before the students left, a television reporter interviewed them. The students said that they looked forward to joining other MEChA chapters in influencing national social policy.

On the day of *la marcha*, the vibrant sounds of salsa music were heard at Meridian Park, and people from across the nation arrived via bus, air, and personal transportation. The Mechistas spotted Geraldo Rivera, television celebrity, and enthusiastically greeted him. Of course, he enjoyed the attention. The Brown Berets, paramilitary Latinos, were trying to get the multitude of Latino humanity to line up for the parade, and at the beginning, no one seemed to listen or respond to directions. Waves of people kept arriving at the park, and speaker after speaker explained why the march was important. As if by intuition, everyone found their place in the parade, the sea of humanity marched toward the White House. A group of military veterans carried a placard with all the names of Latinos who earned the Medal of Honor. Latinos chanted that they were here to stay, *"¡Aquí Estamos! ¡Aquí nos quedamos! ¡No nos vamos!"* At the Ellipse, a park south the White House, CNN and C-SPAN covered the speeches by Latino leaders. The Mechistas were now part of a national movement. We returned to Arizona with a sense of accomplishment.

One afternoon a middle-aged lady came by my office to discuss her progress in class. She indicated that math had always been challenging for her; however, she felt that she could succeed in college.

The conversation changed to current events. Then she shared with me that she was pleased that Mexican Americans were now being categorized as Hispanic. With great emotion, she said she was tired as being labeled as a dumb, stupid, and lazy Mexican. All my colleagues probably heard her pour out her angst. Indirectly, she made a compelling case for diversifying the faculty ranks. I assured her that better days were on the horizon.

On *Día de los Muertos* I was very humbled when a Mechista shared a macabre poem about my eventual demise.

El Gran Escobedo

Aforrado en su porfía,
Escobedo no se fía de nadie.
Es el más genio de su clase.

Y aunque en números es genio
A este sí le fallaron los cálculos
renales y, por eso, la Calaca anda vagando
por los pasillos y canta:
"¿Dónde estás, Escobedo?
Se te ha llegado la hora de venirte al agujero."

"No me lleves, Calaquita," grita el gran Escobedo.
"Si a la fuerza quieres llevarme, primero chúpate el dedo."

Y llorando, la Calaca regresa a su agujero.

Escobedo the Great

With self-assuredness
Escobedo does not consult anyone
He is a remarkable thinker.

And even though he is good with numbers
He failed his nephric calculus
In a hallway, the skeleton sings -
"Where is Escobedo?
His grave beckons, your time has arrived!"
"Skeleton, please do not take me with you,"
Intreats Escobedo the Great.

"But if you must, seek solace for yourself"
And weeping
The skeleton returns to its grave.

My work on the international level began on June 3, 1998. I was invited by the State Department to develop a process to evaluate Bolivian universities and schools.

"Dear Dr. Escobedo:

On behalf of USIS La Paz, it is my pleasure to officially invite you to visit Bolivia in July 1998 to assist the Ministry of Education and the Bolivian Public University Executive Council (CEUB) in their efforts to establish a system for the evaluation and accreditation of Bolivian universities and schools. We welcome the opportunity to host you for a three-week program to be held in the cities of La Paz and Cochabamba."

During this three-week trip, I developed materials related to accreditation. The invitation noted that training and review of the National University of San Simon self-study would be part of the assignment. My initial remarks to the Bolivian educators paid homage to Jaime Escalante, the highly respected educator. The Bolivians were delighted with this recognition of their international celebrity.

The *Universidad Adventista de Bolivia* awarded me special recognition on July 23, 1998. This university is located in Cochabamba, a city with wide boulevards and European architecture. The scope of the work involved *nacional de capacitación para equipos de autoevaluación universitaria;* that is, training of self-evaluation teams of national universities. I was pleased to share my extensive background in accreditation.

Harvard's prominence is known around the world. On August 27, 1998, a Bolivian professor wrote, *En nuestro encuentro en la ciudad de Cochabamba con motivo del curso de capacitación sobre acreditación universitaria, despertó mucho mi interés el poder obtener una beca para participar de algún programa académico en la Universidad de Harvard;* that is, "Upon meeting you in Cochabamba, on the occasion of university accreditation training, I became interested in obtaining a scholarship to study at Harvard University within an academic program." I advised him that most international students received financial support from their government to pay the costs of attending Harvard. I wish I could have been more helpful.

The beginning of a new millennium would be a challenging time for me. Ma Ale had speculated that the end of the world would occur on January 1, 2000; I worried that it could come to pass. The ominous Y2K computer bug was another millennial fear. I knew that most of the computer code was in COBOL and the date field would be easy to fix. I was not sure about the new computer languages that were in play; I do not remember any disruptive Y2K event in 2000.

Dr. Cleopatria Martínez invited me to join the Arizona Association of Chicanos for Higher Education (AACHE). Rising above the urban poverty of the Denver housing projects, she resisted the assimilative forces of American society. I admire Cleopatria for being a stellar college teacher, dynamic leader, gifted mathematician, and professionally engaged *colega*. She continues to be active in the Society for the Advancement of Chicanos and Native Americans in Science. The perennial optimist, Cleopatria remarked on one occasion, "Heaven is on earth. It depends on how you look at life's circumstances. Your glass can be half-full or half-empty; they are both accurate. But there are ways of looking at life that can make it quite wonderful." Her commitment to students and *colegas* inspired me to seek the AACHE presidency.

Elected AACHE president, I was responsible for chairing the monthly meetings and organizing the annual conference, "Thirty Years of *Conciencia Chicana: Del Barrio a la Universidad*." I recommended to the board that the conference be dedicated to Gricelda Zamora Gonzalez, a 13-year-old who died on March 18, 1999, of an untreated ruptured appendix. There were accusations of misdiagnosis by the attending physicians and inattentiveness by the Arizona Board of Medical Examiners.

I requested that the Governor of Arizona investigate this medical case. On March 20, 2000, she responded, "Thank you for your recent correspondence regarding the Arizona Board of Medical Examiners' management of the disciplinary proceedings involving the physicians associated with the Gricelda Zamora tragedy. I, too, was saddened by Gricelda's death. It is unquestionably unfair to have such a young individual taken from us before she had been allowed to achieve her dreams and reach her full potential. However, despite the unfairness, there are simply no easy answers to this tragic loss."

I also wrote to the Arizona Attorney General. I received a letter dated May 9, 2000, from an Assistant Attorney General. He responded, "I have reviewed the boards' confidential investigative files and have spoken directly with the Assistant Attorneys General assigned to each board... In each instance, the files demonstrated that BOMEX conducted a thorough review of the medical doctor's care and treatment of Ms. Zamora Gonzalez." I will forever keep the parents of Gricelda Zamora Gonzalez in my thoughts and prayers.

In 2000 Dr. Manuel de Jesús Hernández-G, a national scholar in Chicano studies, was elected as AACHE president. He was effective in addressing social justice as a policy issue. I felt privileged when he appointed me Director of Government and Corporate Relations. Together we visited colleges and universities advocating on behalf of *raza* who worked in higher education.

Dr. Edward Castañeda, a psychology professor, was a key member of AACHE Executive Board. He is highly esteemed as he treated all the AACHE members with respect and consideration. He was awed by the cohesiveness in the diverse thinking that made AACHE a strong, unified voice. He was generous in sharing his research agenda on the neural bases of Parkinson's disease and drug addiction because he wanted to demonstrate how all disciplines must contribute to an agenda of equity and inclusion. On our trips to AACHE chapters around Arizona, he gave voice to the Chicano faculty and staff at Arizona State University.

Antonio Arroyo was an engaged AACHE president. He was born in Mexico City in 1950 and completed a library science degree. AACHE was fortunate that he created the www.aache.org webpage, and membership was pleased that our webpage gave us a global presence. We were able to announce organizational milestones, scholarships, and conferences. As the AACHE photographer, Antonio documented our meetings with college and university presidents. I was always asking him about newly published Mexican literature.

AACHE voted to support the passage of the S.B. 1001, The Bilingual Education Reform bill introduced by Hon. Joe Eddie Lopez. I asked AACHE members to write to their legislators and the Arizona Senate President. I attended public meetings where emotions ran high for and against Bilingual Education. I made the case that it was oppression to attack a person's linguistic heritage.

In May 2000 I was awarded an alumni award from Pima College from which I had graduated. I was happy to see old friends and former professors. I did not broadcast my good fortune of graduating from Harvard. Yet a former classmate and college math professor remarked that he was happy that I had earned my doctorate at Harvard. I was pleased that both of us had been successful in teaching mathematics.

My interest in mathematics has never waned, and I follow its unfolding advancements in mathematical journals. The Clay Mathematics Institute was founded in 1998 to support mathematical research. This organization promotes research in the seven Millennium Problems by offering $1,000,000 for successfully solving or providing proof of them. The problems are the Yang-Mills and Mass Gap, Riemann Hypothesis, P vs NP Problem, Navier-Stokes Equation, Hodge Conjecture, Poincaré Conjecture, and Birch and Swinnerton-Dyer Conjecture. Grigori Perelman, a Russian mathematician, proved the elusive Poincaré conjecture according to the *New York Times* in 2010. He refused the $1 million prize from the Clay Institute of Mathematics for his work on the intractable typology problem that evaded mathematicians for a century. He also rejected the Fields Medal, the mathematical equivalent of a Nobel Prize. Top mathematicians continue to search for the resolution of these enigmatic problems.

Introduced by Senators Dick Durbin (D) and Orrin Hatch (R) in 2001, Senate Bill 1291 the Development, Relief, and Education for

Alien Minors Act became known as the DREAM Act. This legislation was crafted to allow undocumented minors to obtain temporary conditional residency and a work permit in the United States; MEChA was excited about the possibilities. For the first time Mexican citizens and migrants from other countries, who were brought to the United States as children, could apply for temporary residency. They became known as Dreamers, and more importantly, they could pursue higher education. Yet Congress was not ready to pass this legislation. On July 27, 2017, the DREAM Act was re-introduced by Senators Lindsey Graham (R) and Dick Durbin (D). The Republicans used the Dreamers as a bargaining chip to build the wall on the border with Mexico.

Serving as the AACHE newsletter editor, I found myself devoting more time to writing. I wished that I had started writing early in life as it takes a lifetime to become an accomplished writer. I hoped to become a skilled writer; I always wanted to talk to writers who contributed to literary magazines. I hoped to learn from people who have a track record of writing, and wondered how I would get to this point. I appreciate that writing is a craft that only improves with time and practice. I have found that reading has improved my writing skills. After writing a thesis, I decided to try my hand at teaching.

I was invited to teach writing within an MBA program. Upon meeting the students, I explained that we are all judged by our writing ability; that if they listened to my recommendations, they could become proficient writers. I remembered my evolution in learning to write, and I was determined to share invaluable writing points with students. I started my journey by recognizing good writing. I began the course with a passage of timeless prose, an excerpt from a *Tale of Two Cities*:

"It was the best of times, it was the worst of times, it was the age of wisdom, it was the age of foolishness, it was the epoch of belief, it was

the epoch of incredulity, it was the season of Light, it was the season of Darkness, it was the spring of hope, it was the winter of despair, we had everything before us, we had nothing before us..."

I noted that Charles Dickens, a literary English icon, used antonyms effectively to create contrasting imagery.

Writing starts with a kernel of an idea. In school, we learned that writing consists of an introduction, middle, and conclusion. Remembering a Harvard professor's words, I would write on the whiteboard, "Write in the active voice; tell your audience a story." I noted that it all begins with writing a coherent sentence, then expanding the central concept into a paragraph. Students were required to submit a tentative outline of their paper. Writing is much like building a house; a seasoned writer starts with the initial building blocks of content, structure, grammar, and language. I encouraged the students to use metaphors as they add a luminosity to written work. After finishing the initial draft, students were encouraged to put away the draft for at least one or two days. Then they could return to their work to identify any obvious thematic or structural flaws. I noted that all writers have resources to help them with their written work.

Like any craftsman, writers need tools to perfect their work. Novice writers should obtain these resources before they begin their work. I recommend Prentice Hall's *Writer's Companion: Middle Grades* (1995). It covers the basics of writing. *On Writing: The Informal Guide to Writing Non-Fiction* (1994) by William Knowlton Zinsser is highly rated. Joseph M. Williams's *Style: Ten Lessons in Clarity and Grace* (1994) provides exercises to help writers refine their prose. *Grammarly* is an AI-driven software writing assistant that provides suggestions as you type on a computer.

I wished that Grammarly had been around when I was writing my Harvard dissertation. Grammarly provides a user with writing metrics of productivity, mastery, vocabulary, and writing tone. Writing tone can be broken down as formal, friendly, anxious, disapproving, inspirational, and joyful. Grammarly provides a word count of words checked. Grammarly lists the top writing mistakes. Grammarly features include browser extension, mobile keyboard, native desktop app, MS office add-in, premium checks, and basic checks. Grammarly charges a monthly fee for use of its premium checks.

But Grammarly should be used wisely; it sometimes makes uneven suggestions. If the wording sounds uneven, consult an English teacher to evaluate the Grammarly suggestion. English grammar depends on context for its proper application.

The basics of writing have not changed. I encourage novice writers to be patient with their literary efforts. Writers do their best work when they are fresh and rested. I emphasized that writing is an organic process, and dashing off a 300-word memo in one or two minutes is likely to be uneven and have a few typos. I emphasized the importance of editing and revising. Moving a sentence within a paragraph sometimes makes a big difference in its readability. Revising written work, the writer should find at least one thought, word, or sentence to rework or delete completely.

Figurative writing is a problematic issue; I cautioned students to the pitfall of including clichés in their writing assignments. No matter how grounded in common sense, a time-worn cliché should be avoided. Janet Fitch, a noted fiction author, once remarked, "A cliché is like a coin that has been handled too much. Once language has been overly handled, it no longer leaves a clear imprint." I smile whenever I hear a commentator finish with "At the end of the day..." Every writer should strive to express themselves creatively.

Evaluating the writing process is based on performance criteria. The MBA program had a grading rubric, which helped students assess their writing. When grading student papers, I asked myself, did the student meet the intent of the writing assignment. My first sentence centered on what I liked about the paper; how did it frame the principal purpose of the assigned work. I never was overly critical. Rarely did I start with the observation, "Your paper is far afield from the assignment." I pointed out that no one is born a writer; I provided clear writing tips that would improve the students' writing assignments. In the end, writing for me is a creative process that provides endless opportunities.

The MBA program required students to analyze Harvard Business School cases. The selected cases dealt with decision making, developing a budget, managing people, and ethical questions. The students had to formulate and defend their solutions. But some of the students did not want to discuss the cases, which raised a red flag about their capacity to function in a responsible role. I emphasized that the role of the instructor is not to provide a definitive answer but to help students develop their problem-solving strategies.

I presented a quantitative approach to problem-solving within the MBA program. I pointed out that numbers provide a picture of complex phenomena. I mentioned that a Microsoft Excel spreadsheet can produce meaningful descriptive statistics. I advised students that they must be capable of producing bar and pie charts. I explained that this is how profit centers evaluate their work, and business managers must also be able to make cost-effective decisions. Organizations run on money and someone will decide how to spend it. For the most important decision making, I introduced students to the Delphi method developed by the RAND Corporation. This is a useful decision-making method. For example, how do you make a decision that involves lots of money? No one can be an expert in every organizational issue. When considering a vexing problem, members of the managerial team work independently of each other. Using triangulation and subsequent convergence, they can focus on a possible solution.

Tuesday, September 11, 2001, seemed like a normal school day. Students were quietly watching the national news when I arrived to teach my college algebra class. The twin towers in New York City were discharging black billows of smoke. I was not aware that there were four coordinated terrorist attacks against the country. Many questions were raised about the reasons for the attack by Al-Qaeda. To remember the casualties on this day, I placed a photo of the American flag on my bulletin board with the caption "Never Forget."

On March 26, 2001, I was pleasantly surprised to receive an invitation from the Mexican and American Solidarity Foundation to apply for a senior fellow seminar in Mexico. A former Harvard professor had nominated me to attend the seminar set for May 2-26, 2001 in Mexico City. My contribution to this seminar was to discuss social policy within an international context. It was recommended that my employer cover the costs of this seminar. I did not believe that the college district would support my funding request. In hindsight, I should have paid the cost to attend the seminar with my funds.

On December 17, 2001, the college announced an opening for an administration of justice faculty member. The department wanted someone who could relate to a diverse student population. A Latina, who grew up in our community and had a stellar academic background, applied for the position. She graduated from Notre Dame and Harvard Law school; she had extensive law enforcement experience. Yet the college hiring committee did not consider her qualified for the position. This Latina was not hired for an entry-level faculty position. At another time she could have been a Supreme Court Justice or President of the United States. The paradox of opportunity is the reality that highly qualified *raza* at times are not hired for a job. I expressed my disappointment to the college newspaper and said that questions would continue to be raised when highly qualified Latina applicants are not hired.

On August 1, 2002, I approached Gila County government about establishing a provisional community college district; such a college would serve Miami-Globe residents. I offered to create a master plan for the proposed community college district; I noted that the time had come for Gila County to move away from a copper-based economy to high technology and higher education sectors, which would create alternative jobs to the mining industry. I had observed community colleges eventually evolve into four-year colleges. Gila County government produced a master plan and established a college without my help. While my offer to assist Gila County government was not accepted, Gila Community College was opened to serve county residents.

Perhaps one of the most dreadful events occurred when a math professor attacked Chicano students who attended the college in 2003. The math professor asserted that MEChA was a racist group, ignoring the fact that an Anglo student also belonged to the club. He further complained that *El Día de la Raza* was a racist holiday. He wrongly asserted that MEChA was an active advocate of the *Reconquista* of the Southwest. His emails had a demoralizing effect on Chicano students; the unfortunate coincidence was that his office was right next to mine. As the MEChA advisor, I met with college administrators about what we deemed as hate speech. The math professor was advised that he had created a hostile learning environment for Chicano students.

A divisive campus issue, the controversy pitted students against students as well as professors against professors. The student body president condemned the math professor for his reckless speech. On December 9, 2003, I joined the MEChA students who asked the district governing board to intercede in the matter; AACHE became involved with this visceral issue. With no intervention by the college district, I paid MALDEF $10,000 to fund litigation. The math professor was fired from his position for a brief period. The Court of Appeals for the Fifth Circuit overturned his termination because his speech did not target specific individuals.

Born on August 8, 1947, Alberto Baltazar Urista Heredia, a Chicano poet and activist, contributed his *Plan Espiritual de Aztlán* in March 1969 to Chicano political thought. In response to death threats by white supremacists, he adopted the pen name Alurista. A math professor in an email asked me if I subscribed to Alurista's view, "In the spirit of a new people that is conscious not only of its proud historical heritage but also of the brutal gringo invasion of our territories, we, the Chicano inhabitants and civilizers of the northern land of *Aztlán* from whence came our forefathers, reclaiming the land of their birth and consecrating the determination of our people of the sun, declare that the call of our blood is our power, our responsibility, and our inevitable destiny." I pointed out that I did not write the document and that he should talk to the author; it was a historical document that called attention to documented oppression. I noted that MEChA on campus was founded as a student support group. I have been blessed to enjoy positive relationships with people from all racial backgrounds. But I have also understood the brutal treatment that Alurista spoke of. As an undergraduate conducting research in the library, I came across a vivid account of crimes committed against *mexicanos.* I will never forget the black and white photograph of three dead Mexicans strapped to the hood of a car with white men holding hunting rifles posing for the picture.

At the annual AACHE conference in 2003, I was again elected to the AACHE presidency. Former classmates were glad that I had moved up in academia. My role as AACHE president was to engage college and university presidents on *raza* higher education issues. As AACHE president I would continue to meet with college and university presidents. Occasionally, I would be asked to recommend a prospective candidate for their institution. I recommended a Latino with a doctorate in Economics from Harvard. But he was deemed unqualified to teach economics. This scenario would play over and over. I saw firsthand the paradox of opportunity in effect.

My primary goal as AACHE president was to make every member know that their contributions to the organization were important. The issues that AACHE addressed came from glaring anti-Latino sentiments. At the forefront was the low number of Mexican Americans in the faculty and administrative ranks. I spent my time reviewing EEO reports and the number of Latinos in academic departments. I encouraged administrators to ensure that hiring committees were diversified. During my tenure, I set up a mentoring program for professional staff.

I alerted AACHE to the devastating effects that high-stakes testing would have on students. Arizona had the dubious distinction of ranking second in the nation in the number of students who drop out of school before high school graduation. The Arizona Department of Education had selected the AIMS test — an off-the-shelf standardized test — to make life-challenging decisions. Harvard and the RAND Corporation researchers criticized high-stakes tests like the AIMS test, pointing out that they lack validity and do not yield results comparable to those of the National Assessment of Educational Progress test, which is considered the gold standard by psychometricians.

I was contacted by the Arizona State Legislative Latino Caucus that needed help in stopping the "Protect Arizona Now" initiative that was viewed as an anti-immigrant law. Modeled after Proposition 187 in California, this initiative, Proposition 200, was being promoted by conservative Arizona legislators. Daniel Ortega, noted Phoenix attorney, spoke on behalf of the Los Abogados — Arizona's Hispanic Bar Association — and indicated that legal assistance would be provided to stop the initiative. Dr. Edward Valenzuela, former dean of the Hispanic Leadership Institute, warned that "They will be appealing to the worst side of mankind to support a dreadful course of action."

On February 2, 2004, I reached the apogee of my teaching career. I have always been active in improving the undergraduate education experience. The Secretary of Education sent me a letter of recognition. He noted my participation in outstanding and innovative programs and practices. He highlighted that my work would help college students enter the 21st-century workforce. The letter was an accolade that was an important benchmark in my college teaching career.

In 2004 I applied for a one-year-only academic dean's position. I interviewed with a committee of department heads and college executives. Many of them respected my work on faculty initiatives. After a cordial interview, the hiring committee selected me for a one-year appointment. To me, it was a foregone conclusion that I would be selected for a deanship. HR completed the paperwork on Friday, August 13, 2004.

My first day on the job brought back many memories of hoping to land an administrative post at a college or university. I had fourteen years of experience as a faculty member; served on many accreditation, curriculum, and budget committees. Faculty would joke that I had gone over to the dark side; understanding the flashpoints for faculty, I would be able to steer clear of faculty, administrative conflict. The college staff knew that I hated wearing suits and smiled when I walked by. Every day I would be given an administrative problem to tackle and resolve. I always knew that the true power resided with the department chairpersons.

Fourteen academic departmental chairpersons reported to me. I would relay college issues to them from the academic vice president. I spent my days approving or disapproving budget requests, fielding student complaints, representing the college at public events, chairing hiring committees, updating the master schedule, evaluating faculty teaching, meeting with students, and helping faculty with their curriculum initiatives.

I was most appreciative of the hard work of the secretaries who supported the deans. Day in and day out they would take care of administrative details. Our days were incredibly busy with loads of paperwork. On Valentine's Day, I bought the secretaries roses and thank-you cards. On National Secretaries Day the deans would take them to lunch. They knew that they were an essential team member of the professional staff.

Every year the American Association for Higher Education selects an outstanding faculty member for exemplary teaching, research, and public service. In November 2004 I was delighted to nominate an outstanding faculty member for national recognition who engaged in cross-disciplinary teaching. I noted that the professor used a student-centered instructional approach; I was confident that this professor would make a lasting impact on post-secondary education in the United States. This professor was not satisfied to rest on his laurels; he worked to make a positive impact on students' lives.

It was important to do a good job as an academic dean. A college executive sent me a short note on February 15, 2005. He wrote, "Thank you for all the time and hard work you put into the production of the Kennedy Center Festival. I know that it is a huge and complex event, and you did a wonderful job of pulling many things together." I always had a can-do attitude to my college duties. This was an exhausting job, which did not provide student interaction that teaching did. I worked diligently to ensure that the college produced exceptional academic programs.

As a dean, I was called upon to support curriculum efforts at other colleges and universities. On November 21, 2005, I received a thank-you note from a director of ethnic studies for supporting the establishment of the Ethnicity, Race, and First Nations Studies program at a local university. This program would address social policy issues important to indigenous people. An internship was part of the program that provided real-world learning opportunities to students. I hoped that students would see the value of majoring in ethnic studies.

On December 24, 2005, The *Arizona Republic* published a short piece called *A Tip of the Hat* about my work at the college. The National Council of Instructional Administrators (NCIA) was wrongly attributed to my recognition of submitting a winning entry. I could only assume that the College Advancement office submitted the misleading news item. I only knew of the award when students brought me newspaper clippings. I had not talked with a newspaper reporter about the faculty members who were being honored in Long Beach on April 22, 2006. As a faculty member, I always collaborated with colleagues from other academic departments. I felt that when a new idea is proposed, the faculty should be opened-minded about its potential. My goal was always to implement effective teaching practices. And I always supported initiatives that improved student learning and retention.

After a year of working as an academic dean, I was a competitive candidate for a vice president position. But I asked myself which career brought me the most professional satisfaction. Without a doubt, I missed the students and teaching. Consequently, I returned to the faculty ranks. I was thankful to be teaching undergraduates and working with MEChA students again.

I was sad to learn that Rodolfo "Corky" Gonzales died on April 12, 2005. I shared the news with Mechistas on campus. I remember him as a vibrant political activist and met him in 1970 at a university lecture. He encouraged me to be enthusiastically engaged *en la lucha* — the Chicano Movement. Corky was a charismatic Chicano leader; he was a poet, boxer, activist, and educator. Best known for his 1965 poem, *Yo Soy Joaquín*, he explained the cultural alienation of Chicanos. As a Chicano activist, he was not satisfied with the status quo and was involved in the political system. More importantly, he was involved in voter registration to effect political change. He founded the Crusade for Justice in 1967 in Denver, Colorado to address *raza* civil rights.

On February 6, 2006, I offered to help the Town of Miami develop a revenue stream to turn around the economic collapse of the town in which I had grown up. I encouraged the mayor to explore ways to revitalize the economic infrastructure of the community. I recommended the establishment of a four-year college. In mid-February, the mayor responded to my offer: "I am answering your letter that refers to the establishment of a school of higher learning; I am glad to see that you have an interest in Miami and its economic development. At this time, we do not have the resources to attempt an endeavor as large as the establishment of a four-year college." This academic venture would have been fruitful with help from different philanthropic sources — the Ford Foundation, the Annenberg Foundation, the Gates Foundation, the Carnegie Foundation, or the Rockefeller Foundation to create revenue-producing centers in destitute communities. The mayor and council members were not willing to explore external funding options. If I had the influence and funds, I would find a way to reopen up the YMCA building, which was a community institution for many years. With a $30 million grant, the town could revitalize revenue-generating historic attractions. This historic western town is slowly vanishing due to economic decline. I have always wanted to serve on a foundation board to address community infrastructure problems.

The college district invited AACHE to take part in forming a social compact. To that end, AACHE attended a strategic conversation in Scottsdale on February 14, 2006, and we submitted the policy paper *AACHE Statement on Academic Vision*. We observed, "The exponential growth of the Latino population in the metropolitan Phoenix area is a demographic phenomenon which must be addressed in developing a compelling academic vision. Central to this recommendation is the inclusion of the academic perspectives of Latino faculty and staff." Not as extensive as *El Plan de Santa Bárbara,* we recommended that music departments offer mariachi music classes, dance departments offer *folklorico* dance, and art departments offer courses in Mexican and Latin American art. We recommended that colleges have both English and Spanish signage. We noted that any fruitful conversation must be open to the voices of underserved communities; we were asking the college district to embrace the cultural heritage of the Southwest. Unfortunately, our blueprint was ignored and there were no future meetings to improve the academic experience of students within the college district.

When Dolores Huerta visited Tucson High Magnet School in 2006, she declared that Republicans hated Latinos. Huerta criticized the extreme positions of the Arizona government on English-only laws, bilingual education, and immigration. She stated that students had the right to protest a social policy that did not serve *raza*. The Superintendent of Public Instruction was taken aback by her remarks; he gave public presentations on Chicano policy views, which he considered as hate speech. Open to all students, he intimated that the Mexican-American studies courses divided students along racial lines. He said Mexican-American teachers were radicals who taught anti-Western Civilization and anti-capitalist ideas. Attempts to fire the high school principal and abolish Mexican-American studies came from the far right. Not thinking of *raza* war veterans, critics portrayed Chicano studies as anti-American.

I was home when I got the call that Tío Lalo had passed away on September 24, 2007; I have so many special memories of him living in Las Cruces. He was born in Cloudcroft, New Mexico on August 17, 1930. He entered military service at the age of seventeen and served as a jet mechanic. Later he attended Saint Mary's college in San Antonio through the scholarship program Bootstrap. He earned an English degree and was commissioned an Army second lieutenant at graduation. He was an exceptional soldier who served two tours in Vietnam. In recognition of his indigenous roots, fellow officers called him chief. When I was a kid, he would buy me firecrackers. Later I would visit him after he retired from the Army. Not forgetting his request, I sent my *Tío* a graduation announcement. He loved telling his friends that I had sent him an embossed invitation to my Harvard graduation. In a letter to a newspaper editor, my uncle paid Dad a compliment, noting that he was delighted that I graduated from Harvard.

Silvestre Santana Herrera was a Phoenix resident who was awarded the Medal of Honor on August 23, 1945. On occasion I had the honor of greeting him at the American Legion Post Number 1 in Phoenix; this was the Chicano military organization in Phoenix. *Raza* veterans and families have gravitated to this post for social and community events. Herrera said, "I am a Mexican American and we have a tradition. We're supposed to be men, not sissies." At the age of 27, he was drafted to fight in World War II in January 1944. As a Mexican national he was not required to serve in the military. On March 15, 1944, he attacked two German machine-gun nests. That day he killed many Germans but lost both of his legs in minefields he was trying to cross. A former Army captain, President Truman told him that he would rather be a Medal of Honor winner than President of the United States. The people of Phoenix purchased a home for the Herrera family as an expression of their gratitude for his military service. There are many schools, streets, and parks named after him. In hindsight, I wish I had invited him to come to share his life experiences with the MEChA students.

At the beginning of March 2008, I received an invitation from a representative of the Hispanic Honor Society at the local university to address students on the life and times of César Chávez. I was pleased to talk about the importance of honoring the legendary Chicano leader. On March 31, 2008, I spoke of tremendous support that people gave him when he talked at the social justice demonstrations. I raised my arm and pointed at them and exclaimed, "you are the next generation of *raza* leadership." I told them that my *abuelita* was a farmworker and that she encouraged me to study hard when I was pursuing a degree. I admonished them not to waste their educational opportunity that most farmworkers never have. At the end of the speech, I exclaimed *¡Sí se puede!* The students shouted approval for César Chávez's battle cry.

Purportedly to support law enforcement and ensure safe neighborhoods, on April 23, 2010, SB 1070 was signed into Arizona law. This decree became known as the "show me your papers law" and required that aliens carry documentation of their immigration status. *Mexicanos* felt that war had been declared on them. The constitutionality of this law was quickly challenged. This was a bad law at many levels as *raza* felt that they had become law enforcement targets. Abuse of this law occurred when United States citizens were arrested for violating immigration law. A federal judge ordered the Maricopa County sheriff to stop racial profiling Arizona residents. The judge noted that not having proper documentation was not a crime, but instead a civil violation. For ignoring a court order, the sheriff was found in contempt of court on July 31, 2017. With a pardon from President Trump, he avoided punishment and his civil rights were restored.

HB 2281 was enacted in 2011 to prohibit Arizona public schools from teaching Chicano or Mexican-American studies. What angered the Attorney General and the Superintendent of Public Instruction was that American history was being taught from an indigenous point of view. When I first heard of this legislation, I wondered if the Arizona legislature was trying to circumvent the mandate from the U.S. District Court that found that the Tucson public schools discriminated against Mexican Americans in 1974. I always felt that Chicano

Studies validated students' cultural heritage and recorded the contributions of Mexican Americans. Certainly, a teachable moment, I was able to rally MEChA to fight against racist ideas. The U.S. District Court established that the State of Arizona engaged in racial discrimination when it passed these laws, and found that the State of Arizona had violated the students' free speech and equal protection rights.

I always looked forward to graduation at the college. The college went all out with festive music, refreshments, and appetizers. The students and parents were extremely happy, even if the evening temperature was hot for the ceremony. Donning Harvard doctoral regalia focused a lot of attention on me. One professor called me The Cardinal because of the distinctive crimson color of my graduation regalia; some of my colleagues were impressed while others were envious. I treasured the MEChA graduation stole that reminded me of my humble origins in Mexican Canyon; graduation was a time I would reflect on the sustaining encouragement of my parents.

Every college professor remembers an unforgettable student. Mo was not your typical coed, but an older woman who was an undergraduate. She was serious and methodical about her education. Before enrolling in college algebra, she asked me about my grading rubric, teaching style, and communication skills; she expected top-flight instruction. When she finished her bachelor's degree, she asked me if she should pursue a master's degree. I assured her she was a capable student, and she should pursue graduate work if that is what she wanted to do. After finishing her master's degree, she came back and asked me about working on a doctorate. I answered by saying that completing a doctorate is personally rewarding, and observed that she was a brilliant student. When she finished her Ph.D., I had the pleasure of calling her Doctor Mo.

In April 2010, The Exceptional Students Club bestowed on me the Crystal Apple Award. It was awarded based on my commitment to serving at-risk students. I was ill the day the award was to be given to me by the students. The nomination letter stated: "Students who thought they could never comprehend math were pleasantly surprised to find how they were able to conquer the subject." I felt rather humbled to be recognized by college students. I keep the crystal apple in the living room to remember all the students that I have taught. The best part of the job was knowing that I helped students achieve their professional and life dreams.

President Obama announced his Deferred Action for Children Arrivals (DACA) Executive Order on June 15, 2012. DACA would allow students who came to the United States as young children to avoid deportation and get a two-year, renewable work permit. The president noted that this was a temporary solution and encouraged Congress to enact permanent legislation. I knew that the Mechistas would welcome this change in national policy. Fox News immediately voiced opposition to this common-sense response, bemoaning the specter of Mexican immigration. When it comes to Mexico's poor, it is sad that Fox News commentators take an unbending stance. They have never known hunger or poverty, never read the history of the Southwest, and essentially are tone-deaf to human suffering, or they are racially prejudiced and discriminatory. President Trump ended the DACA program in 2018. But in a welcomed reversal, on June 18, 2020, the U.S. Supreme Court upheld Obama's executive order.

Mom loved flowers. She planted dozens of white lilies in Mexican Canyon that bloom around Easter. Every Mother's Day, and Valentine's Day, I would send her a dozen red roses. And she kept each glass vase. Over the years, Mom constructed a wall of glass vases that framed the outside of the kitchen. I always looked forward to celebrating Mom's birthday.

It was not any different when we celebrated her 90th birthday on August 4, 2012. We had the obligatory chocolate birthday cake with many, many candles. I bought her a dozen red roses, which she looked forward to receiving on her birthday. Mom had always been an avid reader; I bought her a book of poems. It was a wonderful time for both of us; we spent time remembering Dad, Ma Ale, Ma Juana, and Tío Lalo. I enjoyed taking Mom out to Stahmanns Pecans orchard in Mesilla, where we appreciated the natural beauty of the area. Before leaving for Phoenix, I would spend a lot of time pleading with her to move to Arizona. But she had always been an independent person, and she stayed in her home. My happy memories of Mom's birthday would not last.

On September 26, 2012, I received a call from the hospital that Mom was being treated in the emergency room. Her medical condition was extremely serious. The next day, I informed my students of the medical emergency, and told them I would probably return within a week. Rushing to the hospital I could only imagine the worst. When I arrived at the hospital, Mom was sitting on a hospital bed talking to the doctors who were conducting medical tests. She was very aware of her declining health. I told Mom that I loved her. The doctors indicated that the best they could do for her was to make her comfortable. She died on September 28, 2012. For many years I have had to live with a sepulchral sadness.

After the funeral, I returned to work. I could only think of Mom and about the love that she had for all of us. I must have been in shock as I do not remember talking with my colleagues about this ordeal. It was difficult completing my committee assignments. The students were sensitive to my sorrow and for that I am grateful. It has been hard adjusting to this reality, but Mom had a long life, and she made a positive difference in my life. I probably would never have earned a doctorate if I did not have her encouragement. I remember Mom and Dad every day.

Working with the Mechistas was an unsurpassed honor and represented the most rewarding of times. On October 4, 2012, my work was acknowledged by MEChA; this is an honor I will always remember. I admired student commitment to academic study and defending civil rights. Beginning meetings with the farmworker clap was magical, and it reminded me of the men and women who toiled in the hot agricultural fields. The Dreamers who belonged to MEChA inspired us to resist the Arizona government's state action. The MEChA *veteranos* were appalled by the pretentious patriotism of the extreme right. These external challenges to MEChA had a way of reminding me of my obligation of helping them succeed.

My appreciation of Harvard is evident when I worked with Ph.D.s who had earned their doctorates at other institutions. Sometimes I had to deal with difficult people; my conversations with these sophists were always stilted. I always depended on reasoned discourse to make my point. They hated me when they had to grudgingly acknowledge my crimson lineage. But the battles were always about charting a path that would make the college a kinder and productive organization. It was infuriating when they would say I did not understand the issues. I would dismiss them out of hand. I could only conclude that many of them were envious of me.

Over the years friends and colleagues would stop by to talk. A few would suggest that I write a book about studying at Harvard. I joked with them that the experience was probably a dream, an experience that never happened. Many of the students that came by my office were elders and veterans who wanted me to advise them. Sometimes I was asked to help write a funding proposal; other times I would help edit policy papers. I enjoyed the comradeship with the veterans who survived combat. They served their country and had concrete plans to build a future for themselves and their families. One veteran, who was seriously wounded, went on to sell securities.

At the end of each semester, students anonymously evaluated my teaching performance. I was never worried about this college ritual. On the last day of class, I would ask a student to distribute the assessment questionnaire to the class. I would leave the classroom never knowing how the students would evaluate my teaching. The student who passed out the questionnaire would submit the results to the math office. Several weeks later I would get a package of the completed student evaluations; many of them thanked me for teaching mathematics. It was a privilege being a college teacher.

My *colegas* inspired me to work for underrepresented students and staff. I was active in Latina and Chicano faculty appointments and scholarship support for students from low-income families. I found the admonishment of Dom Helder Camara as a way to understand institutional values: "When I give food to the poor, they call me a saint. When I ask why they are poor, they call me a communist."

I hope to return to college and major in Chicana and Chicano Studies as I did not have this option when I was an undergraduate. Every college and university in the nation and especially the Southwest should offer this course of study as a social science elective. Many students wish to pursue this area of study; I hoped to understand my relationship to Mexican society as *raza*. The essence of a Chicana and Chicano Studies program should be the exploration of the lives of indigenous people who produced a rich culture. I would like to learn about life in *Aztlán*; its epistemology, cultural orientation, societal norms, language, literature, food, art, philosophy, mathematics, engineering, medicine, and science.

At the end of a fruitful teaching career, everyone has many unforgettable memories and experiences. Teaching mathematics at the college level was a highly satisfactory experience; I provided learning opportunities for students to be self-directing and developing critical thinking skills. Some of my students went on to become mathematicians. In a Mr. Chips' moment, I decided to retire in 2013 and was ready to enter a new phase of my life. My homes in Mexican Canyon, Mackey Camp, and Las Cruces needed my attention. I wanted to travel and looked forward to reading the winners of the National Book Awards. My students gave me a novelty clock, which had radicands of perfect squares instead of the whole numbers. The academic vice-president wished me well. On May 28, 2013, he wrote, "I hope you will consider part-time teaching and stay in touch with your college family." I never forgot the students who allowed me to teach them. I wish I were still in touch with the Mechistas, but they have their lives to live. I had a hand in shaping the college curriculum and preparing students for professional roles. I encouraged the college administration to diversify the faculty ranks to reflect the growing Latino community. In the end, I was pleased that I had realized my dream of teaching at a college. Now, in the twilight of my life, I have had a chance to reflect on my life and educational experiences.

"Take the initiative in creating your own opportunity. Don't assume a door is closed. Push on it. Don't assume that if it was closed yesterday, it's closed today. Don't ever stop learning and improving your mind."

— Christine Marín, Ph.D., Historian and Archivist
(MEChA Graduation Address, April 21, 1995)

Epilogue

As an indigenous mexicano, I wondered if I would ever study at Harvard. I was encouraged to learn that the Harvard Charter of 1650 gave importance to the education of Indian youth. Harvard archives indicate that Caleb Cheeshahteaumuck was the first Native American to graduate from Harvard College during colonial times; his schooling at Harvard is a poignant account of indigenous life in New England. Harvard has a tradition of supporting indigenous scholars. The Indian experience at Harvard University is noteworthy where the Harvard University Native American Program provides essential cultural and spiritual support.

Being part of the indigenous community at Harvard, I felt that I had an opportunity to conduct ethnographic research on *Aztlán*. I looked forward to establishing friendships with Wampanoag students. Upon graduating I hoped to establish a collaborative working relationship with Joseph Peggs Kalt. He is the foremost scholar on native peoples and is the Ford Foundation Professor of International Political Economy at Harvard. A prolific writer, he has penned substantive nation-building policy papers. If you paid attention to the social dynamics at Harvard, you find *raza*.

Mariachi *Véritas de Harvard*, in concert with the Ballet *Folklorico de Aztlán*, provides Harvard indigenous students a means to showcase their cultural origins. Latino students publish the *Harvard Kennedy School Journal of Hispanic Policy*, which provides leading-edge research on timely *raza* topics. At Harvard, the Peabody Museum of Archaeology and Ethnology has an exhibit on *Azteca* culture consisting of artifacts and primary documents. All these cultural threads gave me an appreciation of Harvard. But in recent days an existential threat has overshadowed life at Harvard.

On December 2, 2014, in a speech at the National Institute of Health, President Barack Obama warned the nation about the Ebola virus pandemic threat. Dr. Anthony Fauci, the renowned epidemiologist, led the federal response and was recognized for his work on infectious diseases. President Obama called on Congress to act on passing an emergency funding request to fight the spread of the Ebola virus. He said, "We have to see it quickly, isolate it quickly, and respond to it quickly." The initial global pandemic outbreak of Coronavirus (COVID-19) was traced to Wuhan province in China.

Harvard University canceled undergraduate classes on March 10, 2020, as a proactive measure against the highly infectious virus. Undergraduate students were requested to move out of Harvard housing and were asked not to return to campus after spring break. While the graduate students at Cronkhite Graduate Center did not have to move out, graduate instruction transitioned to an online platform. President Lawrence S. Bacow said that Harvard would remain open and operations would continue. On March 28, 2020, the *Harvard Crimson* reported, "Harvard College will adopt a universal satisfactory-unsatisfactory grading system this semester as a result of the coronavirus pandemic." The concern was that Harvard senior faculty were most at risk of contracting COVID-19. Forgoing the traditional ceremony in the Yard, Harvard held its 369th commencement exercises using a virtual platform for 8,174 graduating students on Thursday, May 28 at 11:00 am.

President Bacow announced on Tuesday, March 24, 2020, that he and his wife Adele tested positive for the coronavirus. He said, "We started experiencing symptoms on Sunday—first coughs then fevers, chills, and muscle aches—and contacted our doctors on Monday." Harvard alums and national leaders sent their best wishes to the Bacows as they convalesced from their illness; in time, they recovered.

The pandemic sent the nation into a financial tailspin. The national news media reported the devastating financial impact of the COVID-19 virus on American colleges and universities. With bipartisan support, the Coronavirus Aid, Relief, and Economic Security Act (CARES) was passed by Congress to provide a needed $2.2 trillion financial infusion to help corporations, small businesses, and families. Harvard University was eligible for the CARES Act Higher Education Emergency Relief Fund. CNN reported on April 22, 2020, that Harvard University would not accept $9,000,000 from the federal government as it had become a political issue. Harvard President Emeritus Lawrence Summers, Charles W. Eliot University Professor and Former Secretary of the Treasury, expressed reservations about excessive federal spending. He wrote on February 4, 2021, in the *Washington Post* that it could, "set off inflationary pressures of a kind we have not seen in a generation," Still, the nation had to deal with another equally serious matter.

On May 25, 2020, the nation witnessed a white Minneapolis police officer position his knee on the neck of a black man for eight minutes and 46 seconds, causing his death. Reminiscent of the death of Eric Garner, who died at the hands of the NYPD, he pleaded that he could not breathe. The incident set off a national firestorm that profoundly touched Americans. In a letter to the Harvard community, President Bacow reflected, "In the midst of this incomprehensible loss, our nation has once again been shocked by the senseless killing of yet another black person — George Floyd — at the hands of those charged with protecting us. Cities are erupting. Our nation is deeply divided. Leaders who should be bringing us together seem incapable of doing so." Law professors now debate changing qualified immunity for police officers. On June 8, 2020, The Justice in Policing Act of 2020 was introduced to eliminate police violence. Speaker Nancy Pelosi (D) said, "We can't settle for anything other than transformative structural change."

Of the Harvard alums who have a continuing national presence, Fareed Zakaria provides policy analysis on timely issues. He once observed, "Politics and power is a realm of relative influence." As the host of GPS CNN, he covers important evolving issues. He has produced distinctive programming on the death of George Floyd, the impact of the COVID-19 virus on a global scale, and the college admissions scam. Earning his doctorate from Harvard, he has the style of a professor when he speaks. He has written several important books, which focus on national policy. Perhaps his most influential book is *In Defense of a Liberal Education*, which he penned in 2016. He notes, "The classic liberal education has few defenders." But he also says that college graduates should have the capacity to understand conceptually complex issues. At the end of his television program, he selects a book that viewers should read. I would certainly enjoy talking to him about César Chávez and social justice.

George Lopez has given his impression on Harvard, "If you were sent out to search for the changing face of America, odds are the campus of Harvard University would be the last place you'd look. For most of us, Harvard conjures up ivy-covered brick buildings filled with a bunch of stiff old white dudes, Thurston Howell the Third and their lily-white descendants, sitting around some stuffy book-lined club, saying, 'Jolly good tip on that Standard Oil stock, Jasper — and how *are* Muffy and the girls?'" In 2004 the Harvard Foundation awarded George Lopez the Artist of the Year Award; he was surprised by the number of Latinos attending this world-class university.

The Harvard keepsakes that I purchased are tangible articles I treasure. With time, some of these items were lost. I do not know what happened to the Harvard tie I bought Dad in 1989; in 2010 Mom lost the Harvard keychain I bought her. I had my Harvard keychain stolen in 2012. I still have the Harvard ashtray that I had bought Mom. I received a bottle of wine from Harvard Food Services as a gift for graduating from Harvard in 1989; Mom and I enjoyed the Sauvignon Blanc wine on graduation day. Harvard does not permit the sale of alcoholic beverages with the *Veritas* shield. No longer in a hurry, I have time to contemplate the fond memories associated with an empty 1985 bottle commemorating Harvard's 350th anniversary. It seems that these mementos should not be important, but to me they are.

Like many alums, I enjoy movies that use Harvard as a backdrop for a story. Based on Erich Segal's bestseller, *Love Story* (1970) was a hit during my undergraduate years. "Love means never having to say you're sorry," was the memorable line; college students were calling each other preppy. The *Paper Chase* (1973) is a movie about a Minnesota student who attends Harvard Law School. His nemesis was the demanding Professor Kingsfield, who used the Socratic Method to impart the principles of jurisprudence. So true of Harvard, the law students formed study groups to prepare for class. *Good Will Hunting* (1997) highlighted the intersection of mathematics and romance at Ivy League schools. In the opening scene, Matt Damon's character solves a complex mathematical network problem. And, of course, he wins the heart of the Harvard premed student. *With Honors* (1994) is a comedy with Joe Pesci playing the role of Simon B. Wilder, a bum who lives in the basement of Widener Library, who debates a Harvard professor. I am waiting for a movie about a Dreamer from Mexican Canyon who graduates from Harvard and is selected as a Rhodes Scholar.

When Rolegio Reyes was a Ph.D. candidate, he proposed the establishment of a Chicano Boricua studies program in 1971. Other Harvard students have taken up his proposal. Adan Acevedo and Shirley Cardona have established the Harvard Latino Alumni Alliance. Acevedo wrote a compelling op-ed piece *But why are you here?* for the *Harvard Crimson* on May 29, 2014. He embraces the importance of advocating for social justice. Cardona was involved in the Harvard presidential search, which led to Lawrence S. Bacow being selected as Harvard University president. She embraces the politics of interest groups to advance social justice. Both alums support establishing a Latino studies program that will give students a well-rounded education. Harvard students and alums continue to press President Bacow to establish an ethnic studies program.

I was delighted to learn that Dolores Huerta had received the Harvard Radcliffe Medal on May 31, 2019. Her activist background in the California agricultural fields is legendary. She inspired farmworkers and Mechistas across the nation with her unflinching courage. She battled the repressive legislative agenda of an Arizona governor who ushered in bills prohibiting the teaching of Chicana and Chicano history, and allowing Arizona law enforcement to engage in immigration roundups. In the end, federal courts overturned this state action. President Barack Obama bestowed on Dolores Huerta the Presidential Medal of Freedom on May 29, 2012. She is a recipient of the *Orden Mexicana del Águila Azteca* conferred on November 17, 2015, for her service to Mexicans who reside in the United States.

Rarely do I need to call the administrative offices at Harvard. The last time I called it was about my student loan. But when I do, I am asked if I am calling from Mexico City. I did not realize I spoke with a discernible accent; occasionally, I am complimented on my English pronunciation. I always thought I spoke flawless English. Certainly, my southwestern drawl is unmistakable. Then again, I have been accused of only speaking the Queen's English.

Mexicanos are mindful of Porfirio Diaz's timeless lament, "Poor Mexico, so far from God and so close to the United States." Harvard has been a constructive mediator between the two countries. The essence of Mexico is the cultural lineage of its people. Harvard-educated *mexicanos* work hard to contribute their expertise in shaping national social policy. Harvard has been mindful of Mexico's history and cultural significance; Mexicans have established a presence at Harvard through *Fundación México en Harvard, A.C.*, which provides scholarships and mentoring to Mexican students. The Mexican alums return to Mexico to reshape their infrastructure using Harvard insight and wisdom. Every year the Harvard Club of Mexico brings alums together to discuss social policy and hosts Harvard administrators.

Latinos are aware of Harvard's admissions process and subsequent Supreme Court cases. They were highlighted in the 1978 *Bakke* case, which addressed the role of race-conscious admissions. This lawsuit underscores that affirmative action is a continuing legal question. Latinos at Harvard will examine the merits of the litigation brought forth by Edward Blum, a conservative activist. Some Harvard students will worry that they are not good enough, hoping to tiptoe past the admissions office. But after you are admitted to Harvard, and you step onto the campus, all that matters is that you learn the course content and pass the exams.

For Harvard, the trial of the century began on October 15, 2018, in district court in Boston. Citing extraordinary SAT scores, Students for Fair Admissions (SFFA) alleged that Harvard discriminates against Asian-American applicants. SFFA asserts that the personal attributes of the applicant determine the number of Asian admits. Weighing in the controversy, the Trump Department of Justice supposedly found disparate treatment by Harvard. Judge Allison D. Burroughs had the task of hearing the charges against Harvard. Citing precedent, Harvard denied discriminating against anyone and continues to embrace global and socioeconomic diversity as a central goal of its admissions process. The University's internal process was made public for everyone to see how applicants are selected. And of course, critics have deemed that Latinos are unqualified candidates for admissions. Commenting on Harvard's admissions policy, on May 29, 2019, the *Harvard Crimson* Editorial Board declared, "In pursuit of that vision, we reaffirm our support for affirmative action and the positive impact it has for students on campus from all backgrounds. Affirmative action takes a step towards correcting the systematic inequalities and disadvantages present for marginalized groups in our society."

This legal case came down to equal educational opportunity for all applicants. On October 1, 2019, Judge Burroughs ruled, "Ensuring diversity at Harvard relies, in part, on race-conscious admissions. Harvard's admission program passes constitutional muster in that it satisfies the dictates of strict scrutiny." She noted that Harvard's admissions process is not perfect and recommended, "The process would likely benefit from conducting implicit bias training for admissions officers, maintaining clear guidelines on the use of race in the admissions process, which were developed during this litigation, and monitoring and making admissions officers aware of any significant race-related statistical disparities in the rating process." President Bacow was satisfied with the ruling. On October 1, 2019, he wrote to the Harvard community, "Harvard College's admissions process aims to evaluate each individual as a whole person. The consideration of race, alongside many other factors, helps us achieve our goal of creating a diverse student body that enriches the education of every student." Students for Fair Admissions filed an appeal to the First Circuit Court of Appeals. Of course, many commentators speculate that this matter will eventually be heard at the United States Supreme Court.

Dr. Michael Sandel is a political philosophy professor, who teaches a course on justice at Harvard College; he engages his students in a thoughtful examination of affirmative action. When he explores the controversial nature of affirmative action, he invites students to give their points of view on both sides of the issue. And whatever their position on affirmative action, he provides a context of what philosophers through the ages would think on the matter. Bringing Aristotle, Kant, John Stuart Mills, and John Rawls into the conversation, he examines the notion of distributive justice and moral deserts. Professor Sandel notes that Harvard admissions are based on a teleological argument, an argument that is based on the purpose of higher education. His remarks are designed to help students understand how the mission of a university should be crafted. Because affirmative action is founded on serving the common good, it would be a position advocated by John Stuart Mills, the father of utilitarianism philosophy. Harvard University would be well served to have Professor Sandel explain the university's position to the Federal District Court.

Sarzah Yeasmin, in her December 3, 2020, *Harvard Crimson* Op Ed, commented, "'Merit' is not earned, but passed down as privilege. Wealthier parents' children tend to have higher incomes post-college. This merit cycle sustains an admissions system based on inheritance, often relegating poorer students to lower resourced community colleges (if they attend college at all), mirroring segregation in other segments of society and restricting intergenerational mobility. In this struggling economy, limiting world-class education to a higher socioeconomic group would lead to even larger class and racial inequities." Her wisdom should guide courts as they examine affirmative action.

The nation mourned the death of Supreme Court associate justice Ruth Bader Ginsburg. After a productive life, she died at the age of 87 on September 18, 2020. A member of the liberal wing of the Court, she will be remembered for her commitment to civil rights. She had hoped to see the election of a new president.

On Saturday, September 26, 2020, in a Rose Garden ceremony, Amy Coney Barrett was nominated to fill the Supreme Court vacancy left by Ruth Bader Ginsburg. She is a 48-year-old, Seventh Circuit Court of Appeals judge, who Supreme Court observers fear will shift the Court further to the right. Justice Barrett, an adherent to the late Justice Antonin Scalia's judicial conservatism, probably does not support affirmative action. Her testimony during her confirmation hearings did not shed any insight into how she would rule on controversial issues like the Affordable Care Act. She evaded questions posed by both Democrat and Republican senators. On Monday, October 26, 2020, in a highly controversial vote divided along party lines, the U.S. Senate confirmed Amy Coney Barrett 52–48. Like many Latinos, I dread that she will vote to end affirmative action.

Equal educational opportunity continues to be center stage. Amid charges of white privilege, in March 2019, a highly publicized college admissions scam rocked the higher education community by focusing attention on the competitive nature of seeking admission to top-tier schools. As an undergraduate, I did not take the SAT. I would have taken the SAT if I believed that admission to Harvard College was within my reach. I reasoned, how could a penniless applicant compete against rich and socially connected applicants? Now, because of the testing abuses, many colleges and universities have decided to end the use of admissions tests. On January 29, 2021, Harvard College announced that the 2026 class would not be required to submit SAT or ACT scores as part of the admissions process.

As a matter of tradition, Harvard gives the children of alums a small edge in the admissions process. A private institution, Harvard has a historical connection with the people of New England. President Bacow observed that academic qualifications are flat; that is, Harvard applicants have the same academic qualifications. But cultural capital is not equally distributed among Harvard applicants. Coming from a well-connected family makes the admissions process seamless to this elite institution. While many questions are raised about legacy admits, the admission officers stand by their decisions. I understand the argument that advocates make for changing this practice.

Without a doubt, most of the Harvard lectures were superb. Yet they could not compete with an obscure Einstein poster that was displayed in a bookstore on Brattle Street. He posited that "Imagination is more important than knowledge." I always assumed that professors worked to impart knowledge and students studied to gain knowledge. While creativity is central to their work, no Harvard professor ever mentions it during their lectures. I believe that every successful person taps their creativity to construct their future and realize their dreams.

I was delighted to learn that Harvard has established the Achievement Gap Initiative. Harvard economist Ronald F. Ferguson is the director of this project. He hopes to find ways to improve the test scores of underperforming minority students to prepare them for college. Researchers note that there is little difference between racial groups' cognitive levels at birth. But by the age of three, significant differences are observable. Given the underperformance of male Latinos, I am grateful for the compensatory education programs I participated in.

During 2018, perhaps one of the most unlikely invitations came from a Chicano construction foreman in Phoenix. He had 30 years of experience working on constructing highways and other massive projects. We worked together to help high school dropouts learn the basics of the construction trade. Forming a lasting friendship that has spanned several years, he wanted me to help him understand the mathematics of civil engineering. Our solutions to construction problems had to mirror reality. But one day a heavy machinery accident changed his life; his injuries no longer permitted him to supervise road construction. He inspired me because he resolved to deal with extreme adversity with heart and pragmatism. With true grit, he regained his health to assume a teaching position where he would share his real-world expertise with fledging construction workers.

I was blessed to team teach the mathematics portion of GED instruction with my *colega*, Mr. Peña. I was impressed with his commitment to helping students realize their life dreams. We would discuss timely math problems related to the construction trade. Mr. Peña made each student feel special and always had a positive thought to share with his students. He always bought a pizza and a birthday cake for students celebrating a birthday. I miss team teaching with such a dedicated teacher.

Social policy operates in the arena that defines how people live their lives within laws, ordinances, government regulations, and executive orders. My dissertation on Mexican-American leadership focused on four *colegas* who worked to resolve issues related to cultural identity, poverty, employment rights, equal education opportunity, civil rights, political representation, affirmative action, English-only laws, bilingual education, and immigration law. Having busy schedules, they made time to talk to me. I admire and respect them for their courage in leading under difficult circumstances. They overcame the paradox of opportunity, which has been a barrier to *raza* in complex organizations. I am still waiting for the first Latina or Chicano president to move the nation forward. I speculate that it will be a person of remarkable talents.

Latinos must continue to participate in influencing social policy. With the help of the Ford Foundation and the Rockefeller Foundation, Latinos are now capable of effecting change in public policy. The League of United Latino American Citizens, the Mexican American Legal Defense and Educational Fund, and the National Council of La

Raza received funding from these national foundations to advocate on behalf of Latinos. They continue to fight for social justice and champion the Dreamers' wish to attend college. Moving away from its Chicano lineage, the National Council of La Raza changed its name to Unidos US on July 10, 2017.

I was blessed to have renowned professors guide my research. The methodological approach of my thesis was examined by experts in ethnographic research. Each member of my dissertation committee meticulously reviewed drafts of my dissertation. They always gave timely suggestions for my research. They did not always agree with my point of view, and sadly I did not remember all their recommendations, which would have strengthened my research. But in my defense, I had to devote all my energies to undergraduates who were pursuing their educational dreams. These selfless Harvard professors taught me about becoming a college teacher.

I am thankful to my faculty advisor for his patience. Extremely supportive, he helped me with all facets of the dissertation. If the conceptual work were not right, he would ask me to consider another approach. And he would point me in the right direction. He was a hands-on thesis advisor. He assembled a stellar dissertation committee that assisted me in many ways. Emblematic of his student-centered perspective, he gave me a graduation gift. From time to time, I open *Harvard: A Living Portrait* by Steve Dunwell and David McCord. Full of color photographs, this book captures the photographic beauty of Harvard. He graciously inscribed, "With the hope that you will remember Harvard with satisfaction in your accomplishment." To this day I do not believe that I graduated from this world-class university. I find myself wondering if it was a dream; even with my Harvard diplomas hanging on my office wall.

After you finish writing the dissertation there are regrets. In hindsight, I should not have complained that the dissertation was a challenging undertaking for me. Instead, I should have acknowledged the many blessings that enabled me to finish the dissertation. I wished that I had explored more fully the social policy issues that impact Latinos daily. The dissertation was about the challenges that Latino leaders face. From a methodological perspective, I did not fully appreciate the role of money in advancing leadership goals. The saying that money makes the world go round is so true. Every organization has a purpose for its existence, but without money, an organization will have limited success. My research highlighted the reality that Chicana and Latino leaders personally sacrifice a lot.

Over the years, I have been contacted by fledging researchers who have decided to write a dissertation on leadership. On October 16, 2004, I received a note from a researcher from Corpus Christi indicating that she was writing a dissertation on leadership. She stated, "In fact, I want to replicate your study. I am very impressed with what you did, and I believe it's the kind of inspiration we desperately need for the Latino population." I have always been supportive of researchers who wish to add new and fresh insights into the Chicano leadership class.

At the age of 38, Julián Castro emerged as a national leader when he gave the keynote address at the National Democratic Convention on September 4, 2012. Castro nominated President Barack Obama to continue four more years of his presidency. With the aplomb of a polished speaker, he laid out the foundation for a second Obama Administration. Castro spoke of his humble beginnings and the sacrifices that his mother and grandmother had made on his behalf. As mayor of San Antonio, he focused on improving pre-kindergarten education. I was still in graduate school when he was admitted to Harvard Law School. The Democratic base was intensely supportive of his speech, and Castro was perfectly situated to start his campaign for the presidency of the United States.

To the cheers of his constituency, Julián Castro was the first Chicano to announce his run for the presidency of the United States in both English and Spanish on January 12, 2019. His Mom must have been extremely proud of him. Castro's platform supported indigenous sovereignty, justice for farmworkers, immigration reform, expanding educational opportunity, law enforcement accountability, housing for the homeless, and national health care. A graduate of Harvard Law School, Castro was following President Barack Obama's path to the presidency. Serving as Housing and Urban Development secretary he has extensive domestic policy experience. I purchased his 2018 book *An Unlikely Journey: Waking Up from My American Dream* after his announcement that he was running for president. He gives special recognition to his grandmother Mamo, who came to the United States from Mexico as a child. During his time as a substitute teacher, he learned the importance of early childhood education. He spoke of his affection for the working class. He described a steep learning curve needed to be elected and the high cost of running for elected office. With optimism, he spoke about the American Dream in the 21st century. He is truly an exemplar of Chicano leadership. Without sufficient financial resources, on January 2, 2020, Julián Castro dropped out of the presidential race.

Change is a constant in every organization. On June 3, 2019, the *L.A. Times* reported seismic change in MEChA at its national conference. The *L.A. Times* reported that "Today, however, many children and grandchildren of those who marched half a century ago found themselves in a debate over the role of words like 'Chicano' in the fight for rights in the age of Trump." What white supremacists could not accomplish, Mechistas were working to tear the organization apart. At the April Conference, student leaders proposed dropping Chicano and *Aztlán* descriptors from its information page. Central American students felt the organization was too focused on Chicano issues, while LGBTQ students felt left out. MEChA was always at the forefront of fighting for social justice for everyone.

The ill-will between Sheriff Joe Arpaio and the Latino community was at an all-time high in July 2012. George Lopez's comedy routine is based on the hard times he experienced in life. He was representing *raza* when he ripped into Arpaio. Lopez said, "While I am at it, Sheriff Joe go #*&! yourself. *Mas pu'.*" Lopez ridiculed Arpaio for picking on people who could not stand up for themselves. Arpaio responded with, "What is he, a spokesman for the open border people?" Arpaio challenged Lopez to a face-to-face meeting to discuss the issues. On April 29, 2019, the former sheriff issued another challenge to the Chicano comedian to debate immigration. Lopez detested that Arpaio instilled fear into many *mexicanos* living in the Phoenix area. I opined that Arpaio is an intolerant bully who did not serve the public interest during his time as Maricopa County sheriff.

My perception is that education is still a proven way to move forward in life. I hope that *la plebe* continues to explore new academic vistas. There are so many social policy issues that need to be resolved. I am glad that I listened to my parents who encouraged me as a student. I pray that the new generation of *raza* students leverages their talents that give meaning to their lives. The lucky ones will pursue an education at Harvard. They will come to appreciate the value of a world-class education when they enter professional life.

Always the perennial student, I follow new developments in mathematics. I thought that Andrew Yang was making an important statement with his Make America Think Harder (MATH) presidential slogan. I was sad when he withdrew from the presidential race on January 11, 2020. I read the New York Times for articles on leading mathematicians and their work. I recommend *The New York Times Book of Mathematics*, which offers insight into the last 100 years of mathematical advancement. The groundbreaking work of Terence Tao on number theory, harmonic analysis, and additive combinatorics is truly inspiring. He once remarked, "There might be a hidden structure in pi that we simply haven't discovered." This is a fascinating problem that I have been working on for several years.

My circuitous path to the front door of Harvard University was not an optimum choice. I did not understand the higher education topology. I was the first in my family to aspire to attend college and did not get any help selecting a major or cherry-pick classes. Perhaps because I was truly skeptical about the chances of being admitted to an elite institution, where most applicants were valedictorians of their high schools, Harvard was not a viable choice; I did not see myself in the company of the social and intellectual elite. But with faith all dreams are possible.

As an undergraduate, I often felt that my professors provided an incomplete map of epistemology. Rodolfo Acuña — who probably could have taught at Harvard — went beyond the superficial treatment by many academics. His book *Occupied America: A History of Chicanos* provided a meticulous examination of the social forces that shaped the Southwest. Indigenous scholars have an intimate and broader understanding of Third World societies. The aim of social science scholars should be to give a clear accounting of the cultural, sociological, economic, constitutional, and legal forces that shaped our nation.

After a lifetime of study, I believe I would have enjoyed the academic life of a sociologist. As an observer of the social milieu, I found mainstream social science analysis of the *mexicano* community deficient in theoretical validity. Seemingly, sociologists focus on the dysfunctional aspects of Mexican life. In his Yale dissertation *Chicano Social Class, Assimilation, and Nationalism*, Homer Dennis Calderon Garcia postulated that Chicanos have little interest in assimilating into American society. He posits that Chicanos have a positive self-image within a rich Mexican context with its core values. I was fortunate to be able to pursue my interests in the sociological interaction between Chicanos and the broader community.

The Harvard gatekeepers, who work at Harvard, were key in helping me graduate. The professional staff assisted me with many administrative issues. Creating opportunity was the biggest lesson I learned from these wonderful people. I am fond of remembering the Harvard staff who demonstrated kindness in helping me succeed; I was blessed to meet many interesting people. I enjoyed establishing friendships with scholars from around the world.

I learned that you should be an accomplished writer before entering any Harvard classroom. Harvard professors are fair graders, but there must be substance and clarity in your written work. It was a mistake for me not to spend my free time improving my writing skills and reading social science research. If you are planning to pursue the doctorate, read the books I have cited in this memoir. Of course, they are not the only books to read, but they represent a starting point.

Every year I am pleased to receive a ballot from Harvard's Board of Overseers. Harvard graduates have an opportunity to vote for members of Harvard's Board of Overseers. In tandem with the Harvard Corporation, which deals with Harvard fiscal matters, board members meet to establish an institutional policy that guides Harvard University in its day-to-day activities. In 2020, the number of petition candidates has been limited to six, which has caused controversy as to who can serve on the Board. I am happy when I see indigenous alums vying for a place on the Board. I am compelled to compete against Harvard alums who are doctors, lawyers, accountants, and CEOs in the next election cycle.

I still return to Mexican Canyon to enjoy its tranquility, remembering family and cultural traditions. I can almost hear Mom and Dad talking about their plans for the future. When I am there, I am always reminded of Thomas Wolfe's admonishment that you cannot go home again. But much of my persona comes from my formative years in Mexican Canyon. Our next-door *vecino* attended Stanford in 1973 to study business and now lives in Seattle. We all went our ways not knowing how our lives would turn out. Unfortunately, many of the houses in Mexican Canyon have collapsed due to neglect. This did not happen overnight as grinding poverty was a major factor. Unfortunately, I never had a chance to talk to my *vecino*, the late Rogelio Reyes about life at Harvard. I wonder if he ever ate at The Tasty; I was sad to hear it closed in 1997.

Dr. Christine Marín's doctoral dissertation, *Always a Struggle: Mexican Americans in Miami, Arizona 1909-1951* (2005), is a meticulously researched work on the lives of *raza* who lived in Mexican Canyon. Certainly, she described my Dad and Mom's experiences. She observed, "The collective memories of these Mexican Americans revealed much about their struggle to overcome the rooted layers of segregation against them in Miami and their efforts to gain civil rights in the mines where they worked and in their community." She chronicled the stories of families who were forced to move from Live Oak street to Mexican Canyon. My *vecinos* from Mexican Canyon demonstrated resilience to endure life challenges. Having a stellar academic career, Marín established the Chicano Research Collection at Arizona State University. She is recognized and admired for her leadership and community service in the Phoenix area.

I wrote to President-Elect Biden on December 3, 2020, recommending that he bestow the Presidential Medal of Freedom on the Honorable Raul Yzaguirre. His major contribution to the nation was promoting Executive Order 12900 that addressed the undereducation of Latinos. In 1996, he served as Chairperson of the President's Advisory Commission on Educational Excellence for Hispanic Americans. He was disappointed that federal agencies did not substantively address the issue. Six years after the signing of the Executive Order, federal agencies were not complying with its intent. Raul Yzaguirre will be remembered for serving as CEO of the National Council of La Raza (NCLR) and advocating for social justice. I was pleased when I received President-Elect Biden's response on January 9, 2021, to my recommendation. His letter began, "Dear Ernest, The people of the nation have spoken. They've delivered us a clear and convincing victory — a victory for we, the people." His letter ended, "With full hearts and steady hands, with faith in America and in each other, with a love of country — and a thirst for justice — let us be the nation that we know we can be." I hope that the nation supports the recognition of the Honorable Raul Yzaguirre, a respected civil servant.

On January 20, 2021, Joseph R. Biden, Jr. was inaugurated as the 46th president of the United States. I sent my wishes for a productive presidency, "I am writing to congratulate you on ascending to the presidency of the United States. Your commitment to be president of all Americans is an important aspiration." With a focus on positive change, the nation decided to give the new president a chance to restore a semblance of civility. I was relieved that most Latinos voted for the former Vice President.

Even as a child, I understood the importance of cultural identity. I always wondered why anyone should be ashamed of their heritage; my identity was a starting point to understanding my role in society. While students at elite eastern prep schools were learning Spanish, students in the public schools were chastised for speaking their mother tongue. *Mexicanos* bridge two cultures, which produces a hybrid personality. Carlos Fuentes, the eminent Mexican writer, gave a Commencement speech at Harvard in 1983, according to the *Harvard Crimson*. As an undergraduate, I wish that my professors had assigned his novels and essays as reading assignments. At times I have embraced his perspective, "...*Soy chicano en todas partes. No tengo que asimilarme a nada. Tengo mi propia historia.*" That is, "...I am a Chicano in all aspects. I do not need to assimilate. I have my own story." A *mexicano* cannot truly enjoy existence without a cultural compass; consequently, I have always embraced my indigenous and working-class roots.

I cannot help but wonder if I had lived in Mexico, rather than in the United States, how my life would have turned out. I hoped to grasp the essence of Mexican philosophical thought; consequently, I have turned to read the works of Mexican thinkers. A 1990 Nobel Laureate, Octavio Paz is a celebrated Mexican writer who commented on Mexican political and historical thought. Born in Mexico City, he was the same age as Dad, but he came from the affluent class. He served as a diplomat to the United States and France. An accomplished poet, he spent a lifetime pursuing intellectual matters that provided insight into Mexican society. Octavio Paz once exhorted, "Deserve the dream." I hope that I have met Paz's standard by pursuing a dream of studying at Harvard.

With time the Harvard experience has faded into a distant memory. It is still thought-provoking to have a prescient understanding that Harvard would change my life in immeasurable ways. I enjoy reading the Harvard news feed on my iPhone. I read the *Harvard Crimson* and the *Harvard Gazette* to stay in touch with the day-to-day events on the Yard. I look forward to reading *Harvard Magazine* with all its timely articles. I still stay in touch with classmates who lived in Cronkhite. Occasionally I meet with prospective students who desire insight into the Harvard admissions process. A singular experience, I realize that I accomplished exactly what I was destined to do.

Robert Evans, a film producer, once observed, "There are three sides to every story —yours, mine, and the truth— and no one is lying." While inveterate inequality still exists, I believe that educational opportunity abounds in our country; I was lucky that good fortune smiled upon me. In the end, mine was a Horatio Alger story. I always wondered if I was smart enough to study at Harvard and will never forget the Harvard admissions committee that gave me a chance. When I finished the doctorate, I had countless professional opportunities — I had obtained a golden passport to exceptional jobs. I am still asked to join the leadership teams of organizations and corporations. At one time in my life, I thought I could join the Southwest Airlines board of directors.

Dreaming of Harvard has been a lifetime preoccupation. It is not difficult to appreciate why Lewis Carroll felt that life is but a dream. Mindful of my ethnicity, my heart is never far from Mexican Canyon.

I was blessed that many people encouraged me to study at Harvard; in the end, everything worked out fine for me. I obtained a world-class education and my preoccupation with financial issues were re-solved. Upon graduating from Harvard, I found being a mathematics and MBA teacher rewarding careers. I briefly served as an academ-ic dean, which gave me an appreciation of the contribution faculty make in their respective disciplines. I was fortunate that I was able to shift from earning a living to obtaining self-actualization through life-long learning. I learned a lot about social policy that I probably would not have learned in another doctoral program. Life is hard and existence is about struggle; I am still trying to solve the equa-tion of life. Curiously, important life events have become but fleeting vignettes. In many ways, this narrative has transcended what can be thought of as a life lived as an expression of a dream. *Con Safos*.

About the Book Cover

Uniquely creative and beautiful, the artwork for the book cover of Dreaming of Harvard: A Novelistic Tale was created by Rick Rodriguez, from the Phoenix area. The Harvard landscape welcomes scholars from around the world. You can view Rick's paintings at the Roosevelt Row Arts District, in Phoenix. During his undergraduate years at Arizona State University, he was the treasurer of Movimiento Estudiantil Chicano de Aztlán (MEChA). Rodriguez uses crimson and black as background colors for the artwork. He captures the shadows of the ancient city Teotihuacán, near present-day Mexico City. Not far away is Quetzalcoatl. The feathered serpent, a deity in Aztec culture, offers wisdom and compassion to the indigenous people of Mexico.